Edgar Allan Poe

Stories of Mystery and Suspense

懸疑故事集

Adaptation and activities by Janet Borsbey and Ruth Swan
Illustrated by Simone Rea

U0108791

The Commercial Press

Contents 目錄

故事錄音開始和結束的標記
start ▶ stop ■

The Tell-Tale Heart

A classic Poe study of madness and the macabre.

The Masque of the Red Death

The story of Prince Prospero's attempts to escape the Red Death.

The Pit and the Pendulum

Set in a prison in Toledo, towards the end of the Spanish Inquisition.

The Premature Burial

A comic look at the fear of being buried alive.

A Descent into the Maelström

The story of three brothers caught in a storm at sea.

The Murders in the Rue Morgue

One of the first ever detective stories. Poe introduces C. Auguste Dupin.

The Stolen Letter

Another mystery solved by amateur detective, C. Auguste Dupin.

Ligeia

A man remarries after the death of his much-loved first wife.

The Fall of the House of Usher

The terrible end of the Usher family and their ancestral home.

Grammar for First

1 **Read the introduction to this collection of short stories. Decide which answer (A, B, C or D) best fits each gap.**

Edgar Allan Poe's Imagination

Edgar Allan Poe was one of America's greatest writers of short stories. This volume contains nine of his stories which were written between 1838 and 1845 and (**1**)_____ published in magazines. Poe wrote many different types of fiction. In this collection you will find two of his detective stories – *The Murders in the Rue Morgue* and *The Stolen Letter* (originally called *The Purloined Letter*). The (**2**)_____ is considered one of the first detective stories, (**3**)_____ there are earlier examples in Chinese literature. Poe had a great influence on later writers (**4**)_____ as Sir Arthur Conan Doyle and Agatha Christie. He was also interested in science fiction and *A Descent into the Maelström* is an (**5**)_____ of this type of writing. Poe is, however, probably most famous as a writer of dark short stories like *The Tell-Tale Heart*, the first story in this collection and *The Fall of the House of Usher*, the (**6**)_____. Poe also wrote poetry, but this is less popular today (**7**)_____ it was in the past. Poe's career was tragically short, as he died at the age of 40.

1 A ☐ mainly   **B** ☐ readily   **C** ☐ certainly   **D** ☐ definitely

2 A ☐ better   **B** ☐ former   **C** ☐ after   **D** ☐ before

3 A ☐ although   **B** ☐ since   **C** ☐ then   **D** ☐ despite

4 A ☐ like   **B** ☐ good   **C** ☐ much   **D** ☐ such

5 A ☐ evidence   **B** ☐ exercise   **C** ☐ example   **D** ☐ entry

6 A ☐ latest   **B** ☐ last   **C** ☐ latter   **D** ☐ late

7 A ☐ compared   **B** ☐ of   **C** ☐ that   **D** ☐ than

Vocabulary

2 **Reporting Verbs. Solve these anagrams to find verbs we can use to report speech. Then fill the gaps to complete the sentences with the Past Simple of the verbs.**

1 sak   "How far exactly is it?" *asked* the child.
2 masrce   "Help!" the old man _____.
3 lyper   "Why?" she _____.
4 erwnas   "Because it's time," the girl _____.
5 miexcal "You can't do that!" the police officer _____.
6 ryc   "Ouch! That hurt!" he _____.
7 ousth   "Look out!" they _____. "There's a car!"
8 eirwphs   "Shh! They'll hear us," the small boy _____.

3 **The first story is called *The Tell-Tale Heart*. Read this short introduction. Tick the words you expect to read in the text.**

The Tell-Tale Heart is really a study of madness. Tell-tale in the title means something which makes something else extremely obvious: e.g. chocolate around your mouth is a tell-tale sign that you have just eaten some. The story is told from the point of view of the narrator, who says that he has problems with his nerves, but is convinced that he is not mad. He tells the story of his growing obsession with his elderly neighbor's eye, which he calls the Evil Eye. This dangerous obsession makes him want to kill the old man.

☐ candle   ☐ bird

☐ terror   ☐ pale

☐ wise   ☐ free

☐ possession   ☐ anger

☐ spider   ☐ gun

Now read the story and check your answers.

One

The Tell-Tale[1] Heart

It's TRUE! – I'm nervous – very, very nervous. I have *been* very nervous and I *am* very nervous. But why do you keep saying I'm mad?

The sickness had made my senses sharper; it hadn't destroyed them and it certainly hadn't dulled[2] them. Above all, my sense of hearing was better than it had ever been before. I heard everything in the heavens and on the earth. I heard things in hell. So, how could I be mad?

Listen. Listen to my story, you'll see how well, how healthily, I can tell it. I can tell you the whole story calmly, without even the smallest sign of madness.

I'm afraid I can't tell you how the idea first came into my brain, but as soon as it was there, it haunted[3] me day and night. There was no reason for it. There was no anger in it. I loved the old man. He had never done anything to hurt me. He had never insulted me and I didn't want his money. I think it was his eye! Yes, it was this! One of his eyes was like a vulture's[4] eye. It was a pale blue eye with a film over it. Whenever he looked at me with that vulture eye, my blood ran cold; and so – very gradually – I made up my mind. The old man was going to die and I would be free of the eye for ever.

Now, this is important. You think I'm mad. Madmen know

1. **tell-tale:** 這裏指明顯
2. **dulled:** 變鈍
3. **haunted:** 使人恐懼
4. **vulture's:** 禿鷹的

nothing. But you should have seen me. You should have seen how wise and careful I was. I worked so hard and I planned every detail. I was so kind to the old man the week before I killed him. I was kinder than I'd ever been to him before. And every night, about midnight, I opened his door very gently, oh so gently. And then, when I had made a big enough opening, I put my head into the room, slowly. Oh, you would have laughed to see how cleverly I put my head in through the door. I didn't want to disturb the old man's sleep, so, each night, it took nearly an hour to put my head around the door. Would a madman be as wise as this?

My next move was to use my lantern[1]. I had covered it with black cloth so that no light at all was visible. Slowly now, I uncovered the cloth a very, very little. It was important to uncover it so that one small ray[2] of light shone out. I shone the ray of light on the vulture eye. I did this for seven long nights – every night just around midnight – but I found that his eye was always closed. With his eye closed, it was impossible to do the job; I had no problem with the old man, my problem was the Evil Eye. And every morning, early, I went bravely into his room, called his name and asked whether he had slept well. He never suspected that every night, just around twelve, I looked at him while he was sleeping.

On the eighth night, I was even more careful than usual when I opened the door. I felt wise, I felt stronger than I ever had before. To think that I was there, opening the door, little by little and he had no idea, he didn't even dream that I was there. I almost laughed at the idea and perhaps he heard me; he moved on the bed, suddenly. Did I stop? No, the room was dark, so I knew he couldn't see the door opening. I kept pushing it slowly, slowly.

1. **lantern:** 提燈   2. **ray:** 一線光

Then I had my head inside the room. I was about to uncover the lantern in the usual way, when my thumb moved. A slight noise came from the lantern. It was slight, but the old man heard it. He sat up in bed and cried out, "Who's there?"

I kept still and said nothing. For a whole hour, I didn't move a muscle. I didn't hear him lie down. So I knew that he was still there, sitting up, listening – just as I have done, night after night, listening to the mice in the wall.

Then I heard him groan[1] and I knew that he was terrified. It was the low groan that comes from the bottom of the soul. Many a night, when the whole world has been asleep, I have groaned in exactly the same way, from fear, from terror. I knew what the old man was feeling and I was sorry for him, but I was happy in my heart. I knew that he had been lying in bed, awake, since I had made that very first noise. I knew also that his fears were growing. He had been trying to imagine that there was no need to be afraid. He had been saying to himself – "It's only the wind in the chimney – it's only a mouse in the walls," or "What am I afraid of? It's a small insect walking across the floor."

Yes, he had been trying to comfort himself with these thoughts, but it was in vain[2]. Of course, it was all in vain; because Death's shadow was approaching him. Soon Death's shadow would cover him completely and he would be its victim. He knew this – he couldn't see me, but he could feel that I was in the room.

When I had waited a very long time, very patiently, without hearing him lie down, I decided to open the lantern a little. I opened it slowly until a single ray, like a spider's thread[3], shot out and landed on the vulture eye.

---

1. **groan:** 呻吟
2. **in vain:** 徒勞無功

3. **thread:** 這裏指蛛絲

It was open – wide, wide open – and I grew furious as I looked at it. I saw it perfectly clearly – a dull blue color with the horrible film. It chilled[1] me to the bone. I could see nothing else of the old man's face or body, except that eye. I had directed the ray of light precisely, by instinct, onto the damned spot[2].

As I explained to you before, you are making a mistake if you think I'm mad. The only problem that I have is the sharpness of my senses. This became very clear to me the next moment. I heard a low, dull, quick sound. It was the sound a watch makes if it's wrapped up in cotton. I knew that sound well, too. It was the beating of the old man's heart. It made me even more furious, just like the beating of a drum makes a soldier much braver.

Even now, I stayed still, hardly breathing. I held the lantern ray so that I could still see the eye. I held it steadily. The hellish beating of the heart increased. It grew quicker and quicker, and louder and louder every instant. The old man's terror must have been extreme! And still it grew louder, I say, still louder every moment!

I have told you that I'm nervous: so I am. And now, at the dead hour of the night, in the silence of that old house, this strange noise filled me with uncontrollable terror. For a few minutes longer, I stood still. But the beating grew louder and louder! It was so loud that I thought his heart would burst[3]. And now I had a new fear. What if a neighbor heard the sound of the old man's heart beating?

The old man's time had come! I shouted out and opened the lantern and ran into the room. He screamed once, only once. I pulled him onto the floor, and pulled the heavy bed over him. I then smiled, happily. I had done it! But for many minutes, the heart continued

---

1. **chilled:** 冰冷
2. **damned spot:** 引自莎士比亞
   名劇《馬克白》

3. **burst:** 像氣球般爆開

beating, although the sound was fainter. Now it was too quiet for a neighbor to hear. Then, finally, it stopped. The old man was dead. I moved the bed and looked at the body. Yes, he was dead, stone dead[1]. I put my hand on his heart and left it there for many minutes. It wasn't beating. He was definitely stone dead. His eye would never trouble me again.

If you still think I'm mad, you should listen to this. I was so wise when I hid the body. It was the middle of the night and I had to work fast before morning came. I worked quickly and silently. I cut the body into pieces. I cut off his head and his arms and his legs and I hid them under the boards in the floor. I was very careful. I replaced the boards very cleverly. No human eye would know that they had been moved, not even the old man's. There was no blood anywhere, there was nothing to wash, no spot of blood, no stain of any kind, when I had finished. I was so clever – I had used the bath – ha! ha!

I looked at the time, it was four o'clock in the morning and it was still dark. Then I heard a knock at the street door. I went down to open it, with a happy heart – after all, I now had nothing at all to fear. There were three men at the door. They introduced themselves, politely. They said that they were police officers. They said that a scream had been heard in the middle of the night and that the neighbors were worried. They were afraid that a crime had been committed and so had called the police. The police officers said that they wanted to search the house.

I smiled – I had nothing to fear. I said that I had screamed in my sleep – a bad dream. I said that the old man was away on a visit to the country. I took my visitors into every room in the house. I told them

---

1. **stone dead:** 完全死亡

to search well. Then I took them to the old man's room. I showed them his things – his money was still there and all his treasures were still there, safe and secure. I was so confident! It was a perfect triumph[1]! I brought chairs into the room and told them to sit down. I myself sat down; I put my chair over the place where the pieces of the old man's body were lying!

The officers were satisfied. I had convinced them. I was very comfortable. They sat, and while I answered happily, they chatted about normal things. Soon, however, I felt pale and wished that they would go. My head was aching and I began to feel a ringing in my ears: but still they ssat and still they chatted. The ringing became clearer. I talked more freely to forget the feeling, but it carried on, until I realized that the ringing was not actually in my ears.

No doubt I was now even paler. Still, I talked more fluently. I raised my voice, but the sound grew louder. What could I do? It was a low, dull, quick sound. It was the sound a watch makes if it's wrapped up in cotton. I knew exactly what it was. I talked more quickly – more loudly; but the noise steadily increased.

I stood up and walked around. I talked loudly about nothing; but the noise steadily increased. Why would they not go? I walked up and down the room with heavy steps, as if I were excited by the police officers' chatting – but the noise steadily increased.

Oh God! What could I do? I talked loudly – I shouted! I moved the chair so that it made a terrible noise across the floor, but the noise was louder than ever before and continually increased. It grew louder – louder – louder!

And still the men chatted pleasantly, and smiled. Was it possible?

1. triumph: 勝利

Could they not hear it? Almighty God! – no, no! They heard! – they suspected! They knew! – they were laughing at me, laughing at my horror.

This I thought and this I think now. But anything was better than the agony[1] of this noise! Anything was better than the shame of them laughing at me! I could tolerate anything except this! I felt that I had to scream or die!

And now – again! – listen! louder! louder! louder! *louder*!

"Right!" I screamed. "That's enough! I killed him! I admit it! I did it! He's here under the boards in the floor! But stop that noise! Stop that terrible noise! Stop that beating of his terrible heart!"

1. agony: 劇痛

Stop & Check

1 **Are the statements true (T) or false (F)? Correct the false statements.**

T F

1 The narrator is certain that he isn't mad. ☐ ☐

2 The narrator had always had problems with the old man. ☐ ☐

3 Every night, about midnight, the narrator went to talk to the old man. ☐ ☐

4 On the night of the murder, the old man was asleep when the narrator shone the light on his eye. ☐ ☐

5 The police officers came to the house, because the neighbors had heard screaming. ☐ ☐

6 The narrator could hear the sound of the old man crying under the floor. ☐ ☐

Word-building

2a **Complete the table using words from *The Tell-Tale Heart*.**

noun	adjective
	sharp
bravery	
	furious
	careful
wisdom	
evil	
dullness	
	clever

2b **Complete these quotations from the story with adjectives from the box.**

1 "You should have seen how _____ and careful I was."
2 "I had no problem with the old man, my problem was the _____ Eye."
3 "On the eighth night, I was even more _____ than usual when I opened the door."
4 "It made me even more _____, just like the beating of a drum makes a soldier much braver."

Grammar for First

3 **Use of English. Complete the second sentence so that it has a similar meaning to the first sentence, using the word given. Do not change the word given. You must use between two and five words, including the word given.**

1 I had never opened the lantern before.
  first
  It .... I had ever opened the lantern.
2 You should have seen how wise and careful I was.
  wish
  I .... how wise and careful I was.
3 "Did you sleep well?" I asked.
  whether
  I .... well.
4 It took less time to clear up than I expected.
  as
  The clearing-up didn't .... as I expected.
5 I advised the police officers to search the house well.
  were
  "If .... search the house well."

Writing and Speaking

4a Make notes in the box about the events in *The Tell-Tale Heart* from the police officers' point of view.

your arrival at the house	your first impression of the narrator
your search of the house	the narrator's confession

4b You have to give evidence at the narrator's trial. Use your notes to write a full report for the court.

4c Role Play. Work in pairs. You are in the court. One person is a prosecution lawyer, the other is a police officer.

Lawyer: ask as many questions as you can.
Police Officer: answer the questions to tell your story.

Vocabulary

5a Explain the difference between the words below.

1 a watch and a clock _____

2 to groan and to scream _____

3 a thumb and a finger _____

4 a lantern and a light _____

5 a shadow and shade _____

6 to knock and to ring _____

5b Fill the gaps with words from 5a.

1 He looked at his _____. It was nearly midnight.

2 I hate sitting in the sun. I prefer to be in the _____.

3 We lit the _____. It was quite romantic.

PRE-READING ACTIVITY

Listening

6a The next story is called *The Masque of the Red Death*. What do you expect the story to be about? Tick the box or boxes.

- a sickness or disease ☐
- a long journey ☐
- a ball or party ☐
- a murder ☐

6b Listen to the first part of *The Masque of the Red Death*. Are these statements true (T) or false (F)?

	T	F
1 The Red Death was a disease.	☐	☐
2 It was a very quick way to die.	☐	☐
3 Prince Prospero was unhappy.	☐	☐
4 The prince chose the abbey because it was safe.	☐	☐
5 There were no servants in the abbey.	☐	☐
6 Nobody was allowed to go in or out of the abbey.	☐	☐

Two

The Masque of the Red Death

▶ 3   The "Red Death" had devastated the country for years. It had killed more people than any other disease. No disease had ever been so fatal or so terrible. Blood was its symbol – the redness and the horror of blood. It was a particularly horrible way to die.

The Red Death started with sharp pains, then the victim suffered sudden dizziness[1], next came the bleeding and finally death. There was one visible sign; scarlet[2] stains on the face and body of the victim. Victims usually died less than half an hour after first becoming sick.

But Prince Prospero was happy and brave and wise. Half the population of his country had died, but he had a plan. He called a thousand friends – healthy, fun-loving knights and other rich friends – to one of his palaces and there they stayed, safe and secure. The Red Death was outside, but *they* were inside.

It was a good choice of palace; an enormous old abbey[3] on top of a steep hill. It had high walls, but it was comfortable and had been decorated by the prince himself. All around the abbey was a high wall and its gates were made of iron. The abbey itself had a heavy iron door. No-one from outside could possibly get into it. The prince and his friends were safe from the Red Death. When everyone was inside

---

1. **dizziness:** 暈眩
2. **scarlet:** 深紅色的
3. **abbey:** 寺院

the abbey, the servants closed all the doors and windows. They closed them up with iron and everyone agreed that they would let no-one in and would not themselves try to leave. The outside world could take care of itself.

The prince had wanted to make sure that there was no time to think about the Red Death and the problems outside the abbey. He had made excellent preparations for his guests' comfort and entertainment. They had all the food they needed. They also had entertainers; musicians, ballet dancers and clowns. They had everything they needed: the prince's plan was simply to wait, to wait until the end of this terrible Red Death.

At the end of the fifth or sixth month in the abbey, the Red Death in the outside world was at its worst. Prince Prospero decided that it was time to hold a magnificent masquerade ball[1] to entertain his guests. It was a magnificent ball. The prince had decided to hold it in the Imperial Suite; this suite had seven of the most impressive rooms in the abbey. The prince loved things to be unusual, even bizarre[2], and this was his favorite suite. It was impossible to see more than one room at a time, because of the design of the suite. Every twenty yards[3], there was a sharp turn in the corridor and there was another room to delight the visitor. In the middle of each wall of each of the rooms, there was a tall, narrow Gothic window. The windows were made of colored glass and, in six of the seven rooms, they matched the color of the room itself.

The first room was mainly blue and its window was a bright blue color. The second had purple furniture and tapestries[4]. The third was green, as were the furniture and curtains. The fourth was orange and

---

1. **masquerade ball:** 化裝舞會
2. **bizarre:** 怪異

3. **yards:** 碼（長度單位，1碼與1米相若）
4. **tapestries:** 掛毯

the orange light made it even brighter. The fifth room was white and the sixth was violet. The seventh room was different. The walls and the ceiling were covered in black tapestries and the carpet was also a rich black. But in this room, the window was a different color. Here, the window was scarlet – a deep blood color. All the rooms were lit with torches and lanterns – there was a play of light and shadow. This seventh, black room was a little frightening. Not even the light from the torches could make the room less ghostly. In this last room, to add to the atmosphere, there was a gigantic ebony[1] clock with a heavy pendulum[2]. The pendulum swung and the clock struck every hour with a dull, heavy sound: it was so loud that the musicians had to stop playing and wait for it to finish. The first time the clock struck, it had quite an effect on the guests: the pale went paler and even the happiest, wildest dancers stopped to think. Members of the orchestra stopped playing and looked at each other. Then they started smiling and laughing at their nervousness. They started playing again and this time the music was livelier than before. Then, sixty minutes later, (three thousand and six hundred seconds of the Time that flies) the clock struck again and had exactly the same effect as before.

Despite the effect of the clock, the masquerade ball really was a happy event. Prince Prospero had decorated the rooms with gold and bright colors, which added to the liveliness. He was no follower of fashion. His plans were always bold and exciting and he loved color and drama. He himself had planned the decoration of the seven rooms in the Imperial Suite for this particular ball. It was a triumph. He had even directed the guests as to the type of costumes to wear. Some were ghostly, some were very brightly-colored, some were very

---

1. **ebony:** 烏木   2. **pendulum:** 鐘擺

strange indeed. They were bizarre and beautiful and terrible. The play of light and shadow made the scene even more dramatic.

Guests and Prince Prospero himself were delighted with the masquerade ball and they danced from room to room.

And yet, every hour there it is! Every hour, the ebony clock strikes. And then, for a moment, all is still and all is silent, except for the voice of the clock. Dreams are frozen as the guests stand still. The echoes of the clock die away – they have only lasted an instant – and a light laughter follows the echoes as the music starts up again. Dreams live again and take on the color from the bright walls and colored windows. Now none of the guests enter the black room, the dying light has a terrible effect on that particular room. The blackness of the room has a terrible effect on anyone who goes in there. The black of the walls and the scarlet of the windows and the dull sounds of the ebony clock are too emphatic, too sad, for guests at the masquerade ball.

The six other rooms were crowded with people. The heart of life was beating feverishly. The dancing went on and on. The orchestra was now playing wildly and the guests were dancing madly in their bright costumes. The clock interrupted the dance again and everyone stood still as the sound of midnight began. Again, no-one was in the black room, but all the other rooms were full of guests standing quietly thinking, waiting for the clock to strike for a final time. There was yet more time to think while they were waiting for the twelfth. The music and dancing had, of course, stopped and people had time to look around them now. A few people noticed a strange figure for the first time. This figure was easily-noticed, even amongst the guests in their wonderful costumes. The rumor started as a hum[1]. People

---

1. **hum:** 混雜的說話聲

were surprised. It soon turned to a cry of terror, of horror, and of disgust. The rumor was soon flying around the six crowded rooms. "A stranger!" people cried. "A terrible stranger!"

Of course, no ordinary appearance could have caused such a sensation. People were complaining that this was not acceptable. The prince was a tolerant man, they said, but surely he would not allow such bad taste. How could someone come to a masquerade ball at a time like this in such a costume? There are times when people go too far.

The stranger was tall and painfully thin and his costume for Prince Prospero's ball was a shroud[1]. Without doubt, it was a good costume; the stranger was stiff like a real dead body. Most people would have accepted this, but the stranger had gone too far. His shroud was that of a man who had died of the Red Death. The real sign of very bad taste was the paint on the mask[2] that covered his face. Scarlet! Blood! His face was covered with the scarlet horror! His face was the face of the Red Death!

The music had started again, and the strange figure began to dance slowly around the floor. Gradually, the other guests started to dance again, although less wildly than before. They were all concerned and they were all desperate to know what the prince's reaction would be. Eventually, the rumor of the stranger in the unacceptable costume reached Prince Prospero. He heard about the shroud and the terrible mask. He went from room to room, until he finally found the stranger. The man was dancing slowly around the room, making his way between the other dancers. They were clearly worried by him. Shocked and angry, Prince Prospero cried out loudly, "How dare[3] you? Who are you? How dare you insult us like this?"

1. **shroud:** 壽衣
2. **mask:** 面具

3. **dare:** 膽敢

The prince called his servants, "Take off his mask!" he cried.

The music stopped again at the sound of the prince's voice. "You, there! Take off his mask I say! We need to know who he is. We need to know his name before we kill him in the morning!"

But the servants had disappeared. The prince stood in the middle of the blue room. "Take off his mask!" he cried again.

He had a commanding voice and all the guests in all the other rooms could hear him. A few of the braver guests moved towards the stranger. The stranger, in his turn, started to walk towards the group. They stopped still, terrified. One by one, the guests moved back until everyone was standing close to the wall, as if for protection. No-one dared stop him. The stranger walked close to the prince, then, slowly and calmly, left the room. He walked slowly to the purple room, through the purple to the green, through the green to the white and then through to the violet room. Still no-one was brave enough to try and stop him.

Prince Prospero was mad with anger and shame. He was angry that no-one was trying to stop the stranger and ashamed that he himself had allowed the stranger to walk past him. In his shame, the prince rushed after the stranger through each of the six rooms and in his hand his horrified guests saw that he was holding a golden dagger[1]. Still the stranger was walking slowly on and now he had reached the black room. When the prince was three or four yards behind him, suddenly, the stranger stopped and turned to face him. Prince Prospero rushed to attack him. There was a sharp cry – and the shining dagger dropped onto the carpet followed, seconds later, by the dead body of the prince. The wild courage of despair made some

1. **dagger:** 匕首

of the guests run into the black room. They tried to catch hold of the tall stranger in the shroud, who was standing still, in the shadow of the ebony clock. It was all in vain; they couldn't hold on to him. They caught at the shroud, but – the horror – inside the shroud, there was nothing. Everyone now knew that they were in the presence of the Red Death. He had come like a thief in the night.

One by one, each of the guests fell lifeless to the floor. The masquerade ball had ended. The clock in the black room stopped as the last of the guests died. The fire in the torches and lanterns died.

Darkness, Destruction and the Red Death were the masters of all.

AFTER-READING ACTIVITIES

Stop & Check

1 **Answer the questions about *The Masque of the Red Death*. Support your answers with evidence from the text.**

1 What was Prince Prospero's plan to escape from the Red Death?

_____

_____

_____

2 Why did the prince choose the abbey?

_____

_____

_____

3 What preparations had the prince made to make life comfortable at the abbey?

_____

_____

_____

4 How were the rooms in the Imperial Suite unusual?

_____

_____

_____

5 What happened every hour when the clock struck?

_____

_____

_____

6 What time was it when the guests first noticed the stranger?

_____

_____

_____

7 Why was Prince Prospero angry?

_____

_____

_____

8 What happened as the last of the guests died?

_____

_____

_____

Vocabulary

2a Match the expressions using the word *time* in column A with their meanings in column B.

A	B
1 to make good time	**a)** you'll know the result of something in the future
2 to kill time	**b)** you shouldn't waste time, or you'll lose money
3 to have time on your hands	**c)** to make a journey in less time than you expect
4 time will tell	**d)** sometimes, occasionally
5 time is money	**e)** to make time pass more quickly by doing something while you're waiting for something else
6 from time to time	**f)** to have a lot of free time

2b Use expressions from column A to fill the gaps. Check your tenses.

1 Finish that report quickly, please! After all, _____!

2 It's only eleven and we're pretty much there. We _____.

3 I don't go to the movies that often, but I do still go _____.

4 I took the car through the car wash, just _____ while I was waiting for the store to open.

Writing for First

3 Imagine that you are writing a newspaper article about what happened at the Masquerade Ball. Think about the guests, the setting and the important events. Write your article.

Speaking

4a **Work in pairs. Color is an important theme in *The Masque of the Red Death* and in many other Poe stories. Make notes about how and why Poe uses color.**

4b **Discuss the following questions.**
Do you have a favorite color?
What color do you associate with:
- the city at night. Why?
- the city during the day. Why?
- the countryside. Why?
- the different seasons. Why?
- different emotions. Why?

Grammar

5 **Fill the gaps in the text below. Use only one word for each gap.**

The Black Death

The Black Death was a terrible disease (**1**)_____ first hit the population of Europe and central Asia (**2**)_____ the fourteenth century. It was probably carried by insects which lived on rats. Estimates vary, but the population of Europe fell by (**3**)_____ 30% and 60%. The disease, also known (**4**)_____ the plague, continued until the early twentieth century, after which it became much (**5**)_____ common.

(**6**)_____ one terrible episode of the plague, (**7**)_____ 1665, Eyam, a village in Derbyshire, England, became known as the "plague village". (**8**)_____ the villagers discovered that one of them had the plague, they decided to isolate themselves from the outside world (**9**)_____ stop the disease from spreading. Nobody (**10**)_____ allowed to leave the village and nobody came in. The plague continued for more than a year and a very large proportion of the villagers died.

6a Adjectives. Match the word in column A to a definition in column B.

A	B
1 horrible	**a)** uncontrolled
2 ghostly	**b)** exciting, full of life
3 gigantic	**c)** describes someone, or something, you really don't like
4 wild	**d)** very large, like a giant
5 lively	**e)** important, brave, exciting
6 bold	**f)** something that reminds you of a ghost

6b Now write your own definitions for the words below.

A	B
dramatic	
nervous	
bizarre	
pale	

PRE-READING ACTIVITY

Speaking

7a The next story is called *The Pit and the Pendulum* and is set in a prison in Toledo, Spain, towards the end of the Spanish Inquisition. Tick the words you expect to read.

☐ prison ☐ prisoner ☐ death ☐ cold ☐ dark ☐ judge
☐ trial ☐ candle ☐ hunger ☐ fear ☐ escape ☐ rat

7b Poe wrote several historical stories. Work in pairs to discuss the following questions.

- Do you enjoy historical novels or plays? Why/Why not?
- How important do you think it is to understand something about history? Why?
- What do you think the most important events in the last twenty years have been? Why?
- What do you think the most important inventions of the last hundred years have been? Why?

Three

The Pit[1] and the Pendulum

▶ 4   I was sick – almost dead with that long agony. Finally, they allowed me to sit down. I fell to the ground, almost unconscious, but still able to hear the word the Inquisitor[2] said, "Death". After that, the sound of the Inquisitors' voices seemed to become one. Then they became a hum. I could see them. I could see the lips of the judges in their black costumes. Their lips seemed white – whiter than the paper I'm writing on – and thin. They were thin, firm and immovable. They showed no human feeling. I saw their lips move as they formed the syllables of my name. My eyes fell on the seven white candles on the table. At first, they seemed like tall, thin angels who were here to save me. Then, I felt sick when they became ghosts; meaningless ghosts with heads of fire. I realized that they could not help me.

  Then a thought came into my mind, like a rich musical note. If I were to die? Then I could sleep, then I could rest. As the thought came into my mind, so the judges disappeared from view, the candles went out and I was left in the blackness of darkness. I fainted – it felt like a mad, rushing descent[3] into hell. Then the universe became silence, and stillness, and night.

  I had fainted, but I cannot say that I had lost all consciousness. I

---

1. **pit:** 深洞、陷阱
2. **Inquisitor:** 審問者

3. **descent:** 掉下

can't describe it, but I can say that all hope was not lost. I can't describe it, as it's like waking up from a dream and instantly forgetting what you were dreaming. In the return to life from a faint, there are two stages; the mind comes first, followed by the body.

I remember very little, except a sense of horror. This was followed by a sense of being unable to move. Then, suddenly, I could hear – I could hear the sound of my heart in my ears. Then I could feel my arms and my legs. The feeling of terror and horror stayed with me. I could now remember the judges, the candles, the word "Death", the sickness and the faint.

So far, I had not opened my eyes. I was lying on my back and my hands and legs were free. I reached out my hand. It fell on something damp and hard. I left my hand there while I tried to imagine where I might be. I wanted to open my eyes, but I was afraid; I was afraid of looking at the objects around me. I wasn't afraid of looking at the objects themselves, I was afraid that there would be nothing to see.

Finally, with a desperate heart, I unclosed[1] my eyes. It was black, the blackness of eternal[2] night. It became difficult to breathe. I lay quietly and tried to use my brain. I remembered the Inquisition and tried to understand where I might be. The judges had said "Death", but I didn't think I was actually dead. But where was I? People condemned by the Inquisition were usually killed on the night of one of those terrible courts known as *auto-da-fes*[3], and there had been one of these on the day I was questioned. Was I in prison waiting for the next execution[4] date? Surely not, victims didn't have to wait long. Where was I? When I was in the prison at Toledo, there had been stone floors like this, but at least there had been some light. The darkness made me panic. Where was I?

---

1. unclosed: [書面語] 打開
2. eternal: 永恆的

3. auto-da-fes: 宗教裁判大會
4. execution: 行刑

I jumped to my feet and waved my arms around. I wanted to make sure I was not in a tomb[1]. I was sweating[2] in the darkness. The suspense was agony. I moved forward with my arms extended in front of me. I walked quite a way, but all around was blackness and emptiness. I breathed more easily. I was not in a tomb.

My mind was now racing. I thought about the rumors of the horrors of Toledo. People had always told stories about the prisons there. They were terrible stories, too difficult to repeat. Had I been left here to die, with no food and no water, in this underground world of darkness? I knew from the faces of the judges that I was going to die, but how? How and when?

My hands touched a wall. It seemed to be made of stone. It was smooth, slimy[3] and cold. I carefully followed the wall with my hands. It was impossible to judge the size of my prison cell[4], because of the darkness; I looked in my pocket for my knife, the knife I had had when I was taken to the Inquisitors. It was not there, of course. I tore a piece from my shirt and left it on the floor near the wall. This way I could count the number of steps around my cell. I continued my slow walk around. The floor was slimy too and, at one point, I fell. I was exhausted, so I fell into a deep sleep.

When I woke up, I put out my arm and found that there was some bread and water next to me. I didn't think about why this had happened at the time, I just ate and drank. Then I walked around the wall again, until I found my piece of shirt. I counted my steps. One hundred; my prison was one hundred steps around. There was no point in[5] doing this, except curiosity.

Now I decided to leave the wall and cross into the center of the

---

1. **tomb:** 墳墓
2. **sweating:** 流汗
3. **slimy:** 黏滑的
4. **cell:** 牢房
5. **no point in:** 沒道理

room. I was careful, because the floor was so slimy. I went forward ten steps, but then I fell again. There was a strange smell of fungus[1]. I put out my hand. I had fallen at the edge of a circular pit. I found a small piece of stone and dropped it into the pit. I listened for a long time, then I heard it. I heard the splash of water. At the same time, a door opened somewhere above my head and light flashed through the gloom[2] and then quickly faded away.

I saw clearly how they planned to kill me. I was lucky. If I hadn't fallen over, I would have fallen into the pit and died. This was one of the stories I had heard about the Inquisition. There was a choice of deaths. Death with terrible physical agony or death with terrible mental horrors. I was going to suffer the second. I was shaking.

Again, I fell asleep and when I woke, there was bread and water next to me. I drank the water, but they must have put something in it. I fell asleep. When I woke up and unclosed my eyes, it was light. I could now see the extent of my prison cell. It was smaller than I had thought. It was square. There were metal plates on the walls with images of death and destruction. I could see the pit in the floor.

It was difficult to look around me, because I was now lying on my back. I was on a wooden board. There were ropes around me and so I was tied to the board. I could just move my left arm, so I could feed myself. There was no water. This terrified me, as the food was very salty and I was thirsty.

I looked up at the high ceiling. Directly above me was the image of Time. He was holding a huge pendulum. I looked more closely. The pendulum was actually a blade[3] and it was moving. The movement was slow, very slow.

I heard a noise beside me and looked down in horror. Rats.

---

1. **fungus:** 菌類
2. **gloom:** 陰暗

3. **blade:** 刀鋒

Enormous rats were coming out of the pit. Of course, they were attracted by the smell of the meat. I worked hard to scare them away.

I looked up again, the pendulum was moving faster. It was also moving downwards. Oh, the horror. The horror of the razor-sharp blade. The horror of the hissing[1] sound it made as it moved through the air.

Oh, the agents of the Inquisition! The intelligence and ingenuity of their methods of torture[2]! The agents of the Inquisition knew that *I* knew about the pit. The pit had been designed as a symbol of hell. Now it seemed they had planned a different method of execution for me.

There is no reason to talk about the long, long hours of horror. I counted the movement of the pendulum. It seemed like ages, but down and down it came! Days passed, it might have been many days. Sometimes I was mad. Sometimes I was calm. Finally, I fainted.

I don't know how long I was unconscious, but when I woke up, I was sick and weak. I picked up the last piece of food. The rats had eaten the rest. I had the beginnings of an idea.

Down came the pendulum. Down came the blade.

Now it was swinging very near to my chest. I tried in vain to free my other arm. If I could do that, then, at least, I could try to escape.

Down, without slowing, came the pendulum and its razor-sharp blade.

My eyes followed every swing. Could it be slowing? Would it stop? I still had hope. Perhaps the machine would break down. Hope never dies, not even in the prisons of the Inquisition.

Now I could see that I had very little time until the blade started to cut my shirt. Suddenly, I was calm. This was the end. There were too many ropes around me. The pendulum would cut some of them, but not all of them.

---

1. **hissing:** 嘶嘶聲   2. **torture:** 折磨

I returned to the half idea I had had earlier, when I was thinking about the food and the rats. There were now more rats than before. Perhaps they were waiting for *me* to become their food. I still had one small piece of meat. My idea was this: I decided to spread it over as many of the ropes around me as I could. Perhaps it would work.

The pendulum was now too close. This was my last chance. I was lucky; the rats were hungry. In a few seconds, my ropes were covered in the horrid creatures. They chewed at the ropes, desperate for the meat. Soon, there were hundreds of them. Disgusting, hungry creatures. They weren't disturbed by the swinging of the pendulum. They pressed down on me, they chewed and then suddenly, I could feel the ropes were less tight. I lay still.

At last, I knew I was free, but the pendulum had now cut my shirt. I waited until its high point and quickly I got off the board onto the floor. Free! But still in the hands of the Inquisition.

As soon as I stood up, the motion of the pendulum stopped and it started to move upwards. An invisible force was moving it upwards. I knew I was being watched. I had escaped death in one way, but it would come to me in another.

I was right, the walls of my prison cell started to move. The metal plates on the wall! They were making my prison smaller, minute by minute. For some reason, the Inquisitors now had no time to waste. I hadn't fallen into the pit, I had escaped the pendulum, now the walls of the cell were going to close in and push me into the deep, dark, horrifying abyss[1] in the middle of the cell.

It was so warm and there was a terrible smell of hot iron. The walls were coming nearer. Again, they wanted me to choose; this

---

1. **abyss:** 無底洞

time I had to choose between the hot iron of the walls and the cool water of the pit. I had no time. Despair. The walls were closing fast. I had seconds to live. This time there was no escape. I let out one last, final scream of despair, I closed my eyes –

There was a hum, a hum of human voices! There was a sound, like the sound of trumpets! There was a sound of metal on metal! The walls rushed back! A hand caught mine, as I fainted. A hand saved me from the pit. It was the hand of General Lasalle. The French army had entered Toledo. The Inquisition had ended.

Stop & Check

1 **Put these nine events into the order they appear in *The Pit and the Pendulum*.**

1 ☐ After waking up, he finds himself tied to a wooden board with the pendulum high above him

2 ☐ Rats eat his food and the ropes around him

3 ☐ Finally, the narrator is freed when the French army enters Toledo and ends the Inquisition

4 ☐ He walks across his cell and finds a pit in the center

5 ☑ First of all, the narrator appears in front of the judges of the Inquisition

6 ☐ The pendulum is about to kill him when he breaks free

7 ☐ The hot walls of the cell begin to close around him; he will be pushed into the pit or die from the heat of the walls

8 ☐ He collapses into unconsciousness for the first time

9 ☐ He walks around the walls of his cell to see how large it is

Word-building

2a **Complete the table of crime words. Use your dictionary to help you.**

crime	criminal	verb(s)
homicide		to murder/to kill
	thief	
	fraudster	to defraud
blackmail		
	arsonist	to set fire to
	rapist	
shoplifting		
burglary		
	robber	to rob

2b Work in pairs. Talk about appropriate punishments for the crimes in 2a. Use the words in the box or add your own ideas. Use your dictionary to help you.

> a life sentence • a fine • community service
>
> a caution • a prison sentence

Reading for First

3 Look again at pages 32 and 33. Choose the answer (A, B, C or D) which you think fits best according to the text.

1 What was the narrator's initial thought when he saw the candles?
  A They were angels.
  B They were ghosts.
  C They were condemning him.
  D They were meaningless.

2 What did the narrator mean by "a mad, rushing descent into hell"?
  A The judges had all rushed away at the end of the trial.
  B The candles had all suddenly gone out.
  C He was quickly losing consciousness.
  D He had died.

3 How did the narrator describe recovering from a faint?
  A Like regaining hope.
  B Like waking up after a dream.
  C Like losing all hope.
  D Like a feeling of horror.

4 Why didn't the narrator want to open his eyes?
  A He was afraid of the objects that might be in the room.
  B He didn't want to see the judges again.
  C He was worried that he would be tied up.
  D He was afraid that there would be nothing there.

5 The narrator thought
  A that he wasn't dead.
  B that he was waiting for the next *auto-da-fé*.
  C that he was still in the room with the judges.
  D that he was in the same prison cell in Toledo as before.

Vocabulary and Speaking

4a **Match these onomatopoeic words to their definitions.**

1 hiss   ☐   **a)** the sound of lots of people talking normally

2 tick   ☐   **b)** the sound a balloon makes when you burst it

3 clang   ☐   **c)** the sound water makes

4 splash   ☐   **d)** the sound a bell makes

5 hum   ☐   **e)** the sound a snake makes

6 pop   ☐   **f)** the sound a clock makes

4b **Fill the gaps using words from 4a.**

1 The _____ing sound reminded her it was almost time to leave.

2 There was a _____ as they jumped into the sea.

3 The _____ of their voices could be heard from the other room.

4 It was impossible to hear yourself think over the _____ing as Big Ben struck twelve.

4c **Work in pairs. Discuss these questions.**

- What's the most annoying sound you can think of? Why?
- What's the nicest sound you know? Why?
- Is there a sound that reminds you of childhood?
- Are there any cases when noise should be limited? What are they?

Grammar

5 **Complete the text about the Spanish Inquisition, using connectors from the box. Then answer the questions.**

> although • in spite of • however

The Spanish Inquisition

The Inquisition was a court of the Catholic church. Its name comes from the Latin term *Inquisitio* which means investigation or inquiry. It was used to investigate cases of heresy (actions or beliefs which were against official church policy). **(1)**_____ it started in the twelfth century, it became much more prominent in the fifteenth century. There were a number of different punishments, such as prayer, imprisonment or execution. The Inquisition was used in Italy and France and then, in 1478, it was authorized in Spain. (**2**)_____this authorization, the Pope soon tried to limit the powers of the Spanish Inquisition. This was because it was used by the monarchy for political reasons. The Grand Inquisitor in Spain was Tomás de Torquemada. He was the organizer of the *autos-da-fé* – the public court for heretics. Many heretics were tried by the Inquisition and about 2,000 were executed in Spain. The Spanish Inquisition was also introduced into other Spanish territories such as Mexico, Peru, Sicily and the Netherlands, but began to lose power in the sixteenth century. It continued, (**3**)_____, in Spain until the nineteenth century.

1 When did the Inquisition start? _____
2 When did the Spanish Inquisition start? _____
3 What was the name of the court procedure? _____
4 Why was the Inquisition introduced into Mexico and Sicily?_____
5 When did the Spanish Inquisition end? _____

PRE-READING ACTIVITY

Vocabulary and Speaking

6a **The name of the next story is *The Premature Burial*. Match the words in column A with those with similar meanings in column B. Use your dictionary to help you. Check with your partner.**

A	B
1 grave (n)	**a)** worried (adj)
2 research (n)	**b)** cover (n)
3 blackness (n)	**c)** tomb (n)
4 cemetery (n)	**d)** early (adj)
5 tired (adj)	**e)** graveyard (n)
6 lid (n)	**f)** dark (n)
7 premature (adj)	**g)** exhausted (adj)
8 uneasy (adj)	**h)** investigation (n)

6b **The last line in the story is *"I learnt a valuable lesson: we must overcome our fears. They must be put to sleep or else we die."* Work in pairs. Discuss: what do you think Poe means by this?**

Four

The Premature Burial

▶ 5 Terrible things happen in the world, but the worst thing that can happen to an individual is to be buried alive. There is such a fine line between life and death. Who knows where one ends and the other begins? There are some diseases where the person appears to be dead, but is, in fact, in a deep coma. After a certain amount of time, the person comes back to life. Where, in the meantime, was the soul?

Medical professionals and ordinary people all have stories of premature burial. I could easily tell you about a hundred cases.

There was one which some of my readers may remember. It was in all the newspapers in the country. The wife of one of the most respected citizens of Baltimore – a lawyer and member of Congress – was taken sick. The doctors were unable to help her. She suffered greatly and then she died, or at least, everyone thought she had died. She looked like she was dead. Her skin was cold, her lips were bloodless and her eyes were dry. For three days, the body lay in its coffin[1], stiff and cold in its shroud.

The lady was placed in the family tomb[2]. The tomb was next opened three years later, for the burial of another family member.

---

1. **coffin:** 棺材　　　　　　　2. **family tomb:** 家族墓地

The husband had a terrible shock when he opened the door and the skeleton of his wife fell into his arms.

There was an investigation. It was clear that the poor woman had woken up from her "death". Her coffin had fallen from its shelf and opened. There were signs that she had tried to break down the heavy iron door of the family tomb. Somehow, her shroud had become caught on the door. That was why her skeleton had fallen into her husband's arms, as soon as he had opened the door. The poor lady had probably died of terror.

There is another story from the year 1810, in France. Mademoiselle Victorine Lafourcade was a beautiful wealthy[1] young woman from a very good family. She had many offers of marriage. One man who wanted to marry her was Julien Bossuet, a poor writer from Paris. She loved him and he loved her, but family honor led her to marry a Monsieur Renelle, an important banker and diplomat[2]. The marriage was not happy; indeed there were rumors that he treated her very badly. She died or, once again, everyone thought she had died. She was buried in a grave, not in a family tomb. The lover, Bossuet, traveled from Paris with the romantic idea of being buried in the same grave. He dug the earth from the grave and found the coffin. He opened it up and looked at his love. Her eyes suddenly opened!

To cut a long story short, she had not died, although she had been sick for a long time and her sickness had made her pale, thin and cold. Bossuet looked after Victorine, in secret, and she eventually recovered. They decided not to tell her family as, under French law, she would have had to return to her husband. The lovers escaped to America where they lived happily for twenty years. They eventually

---

1. **wealthy:** 富有　　　　　2. **diplomat:** 外交家

returned to Paris, convinced that no-one would recognize them. Unfortunately, Monsieur Renelle immediately recognized his wife and went to the court to force Victorine to return to him. The court, however, decided that the very unusual circumstances meant that the marriage was over: the lovers were free to stay together.

Another important case happened in Germany. An army officer – tall and strong – was thrown from his horse. The doctors were sure he would make a complete recovery. They were wrong, the man got worse and worse, until he apparently died. The weather was warm, so he was buried very quickly, on a Thursday. The following Sunday, there were a lot of visitors at the cemetery, as usual. One man felt movement in the earth as he walked near the officer's grave. The crowd dug up the coffin, and there the officer was, in a sitting position. He was taken to the nearest hospital. Although he survived being buried alive, he was treated by the worst kind of doctors. Unfortunately, these "medical professionals" killed him.

Talking of medical professionals, there was another case in London, where a young man called Mr. Edward Stapleton had apparently died. This time, the body was dug up by body-snatchers – those terrible criminals who dig up the bodies of dead people and sell them to doctors for medical research. Mr. Stapleton was very lucky, because the medical students were experimenting with batteries. They applied a battery charge to Mr. Stapleton's heart and were shocked themselves when he sat up. He is now alive and well and still living in London.

★★★

It would be easy to tell a hundred stories like this, but now it's time to tell you about my own experience. I had, for many years, been afraid of the idea of being buried alive. I was afraid of the blackness, of being covered with earth, of the horror of being under the ground. My situation was unusual, as I suffered from a terrible sickness called catalepsy[1]. Now catalepsy is a strange sickness. No-one understands the cause, but cataleptics often suffer apparent death. We lie still, it's difficult to feel our heart beat and there is very little color in our cheeks and lips. Our family and friends know that we are cataleptic so, if we are lucky, they can save us from premature burial. The cataleptic state can last for a day or for months.

I myself had two types of cataleptic attack. Sometimes I was simply tired and without any energy. I would stay in bed until the crisis passed. Then I would be fine again. The other type was more serious; I would be sick, then chilled to the bone, then dizzy. In these cases, everything would be black and silent for weeks. The universe became nothing. Then, eventually, my soul would come back to me, although I would be confused for a short time.

My general health was very good, but I was terrified of the idea of a premature burial. I called it the Danger. I was obsessed by Death and Darkness. When I slept, I dreamt of Death and Ghosts. Gradually, this began to affect my life. It was impossible to sleep, I was afraid of riding or walking. I told all my friends about my fears. "When I die, you must leave my body in an open coffin."

"Why?" they asked.

"I must never be buried alive. You must be totally sure that I am dead. I must not be put into the family tomb until you are absolutely certain that I am stone dead."

1. **catalepsy:** 全身僵硬症

They laughed at my fears.

It was obvious to me that further preparations were needed. I decided to make some alterations to the family tomb. I had the door changed so that it was possible to open it from the inside. I made sure that there was plenty of air and light inside the tomb. My coffin was extremely comfortable. The lid was easy to open. There were containers for food and water near the coffin and there was also a large bell. It was designed so that the rope came into the coffin, so that I could ring it, if necessary. All possible preparations had been made; I would be able to escape, or call for help, if I were buried prematurely during one of my cataleptic attacks.

***

One day, it happened. I found myself coming out of total unconsciousness into the first sense of existence. I was anxious. I could hear a ringing sound in my ears. Then, little by little, I began to be able to feel my fingers, then my hands and then my feet. I was exhausted and I fell asleep again, then suddenly I woke up. I had recovered. I had obviously been sick. I felt an electric shock of terror. I couldn't remember! Why couldn't I remember? Where was I? I felt that I was not waking up from ordinary sleep. It had been an attack of catalepsy. The Danger. I remembered the Danger.

I couldn't move. I was afraid to move, afraid to try. I opened my eyes. It was dark – all dark. It was the intense darkness of eternal Night. I tried to shout, but no noise came out. My chest felt as if it had the weight of a mountain on it. I was lying on a hard surface and

I could feel wood against my sides. I threw up my arms. They hit wood. There was no doubt, I was lying in my coffin. But why was I not comfortable? My coffin was supposed to be comfortable.

In my fear, I found Hope. I suddenly remembered the bell. I felt around for the rope. I could pull the rope and then my friends and family would hear the bell. They would come running to the family tomb, force open the door and take me out of my coffin.

After Hope came Despair. This wasn't *my* coffin! It was uncomfortable, there was no rope. There was no rope, so there was no bell. I was sweating as I began to understand what had happened. Clearly I had fallen sick when I was away from home; away from my family and friends. I had had a cataleptic attack when I was with strangers. They had thought that I was dead. Why wouldn't they? Strangers had buried me deep, deep in the earth. I screamed. My long, wild, continuous scream sounded through the Night.

"Hey!" said a voice, in reply.

"What's going on?" said a second.

"Stop that noise!" said a third.

"What are you screaming about?" said a fourth.

Someone was shaking me. They were shaking me quite violently, too. Who was it? Where was I?

I sat up and looked around me. There were four people and myself. Memory flooded back.

I was near Richmond, Virginia. I was traveling with four of my friends. We were on a sailing expedition on the James River. We were in the cabin of a small boat. Of course, the beds were very narrow, as they always are on a boat. We had been complaining about how uncomfortable they were. The beds also had sides, to stop people from falling out in bad weather. I had woken my four friends up, in the middle of the night, with my scream of fear at the idea of being buried alive. My friends were now laughing at me.

The experience changed my life. I breathed the free air of Heaven. I thought about other things rather than Death. I gave away my medical books. I gave away all books with stories of premature burial, nightmares and horrors. I took exercise, I traveled; in short, I became a new man.

Strangely enough, my catalepsy disappeared. Perhaps it wasn't so strange, as I began to understand that my sickness had been caused by my fears, not the other way round as I had thought. As a result of my stupidity, I learnt a valuable lesson: we must overcome our fears. They must be put to sleep or else we die.

Stop & Check

1 **Who did these things happen to in *The Premature Burial*?**

Choose from:
A The narrator
B The wife of the famous lawyer
C Victorine Lafourcade
D Edward Stapleton

Which person:
a) ☐ was saved by a man who loved her?
b) ☐ was saved by body-snatchers and medical students?
c) ☐ was terrified of being buried alive?
d) ☐ probably died of terror?
e) ☐ pretended to be dead after being saved from the tomb?
f) ☐ died in the family tomb?
g) ☐ was obsessed by Death and Darkness?
h) ☐ was not put in a tomb or coffin when they were alive?
i) ☐ had a violent husband?
j) ☐ was alive and well and living in London?
k) ☐ went to live in Paris?
l) ☐ overcame a fear?

2 **Look again at the first page of *The Premature Burial*. Find words/phrases that mean the same as the words/phrases below. The words are in the same order in the text.**

1 dreadful _____
2 living _____
3 sicknesses _____
4 during that time _____
5 looked up to _____
6 rigid _____

Writing

3 Write about a frightening experience you have had. Organize your writing into paragraphs. Use a selection of the following sequencers.

> first of all • at first • after that • then • after a short time
> not long after • quite soon after • finally

Grammar for First

4 Read the text below and think of the word which best fits each gap. Use only **one** word in each gap.

Catalepsy

Catalepsy is a symptom of a number (**1**)_____ medical conditions, often nervous disorders. It can appear suddenly (**2**)_____ warning. Patients seem to be unconscious, (**3**)_____ they may be aware of their surroundings. Patients' arms and legs are stiff and they do not respond when people speak (**4**)_____ them. Sometimes people can be put into a cataleptic state (**5**)_____ hypnotists.

There are many references to catalepsy in literature. Edgar Allan Poe used it in *The Premature Burial*, written in 1844, and in other short stories. Other writers (**6**)_____ as Tennyson, Alexandre Dumas, Emile Zola and Charles Dickens referred to cataleptic states. Nineteenth century writers and readers alike were fascinated (**7**)_____ the subject and by the possibility of people being buried when they were still alive.

Cataleptic states can also be brought on by a bad shock. One example of this comes (**8**)_____ sport. Bob Beamon is a former American long jumper. He was competing in the 1968 Olympic Games in Mexico, when he broke the world record by (**9**)_____ incredible half a metre. For a few minutes, Beamon was unable to move, (**10**)_____ to the extreme shock of his enormous jump.

Word-building

5a Prefixes. Use prefixes from the box to build the opposites of these adjectives. Check your answers in a dictionary.

un-	im-	in-	il-	ir-

1 _un_comfortable

2 ___able

3 ___relevant

4 ___logical

5 ___fortunate

6 ___edible

7 ___rational

8 ___literate

9 ___conscious

10 ___patient

5b Rewrite these sentences using one of the adjectives from 5a.

1 There was too much salt in the soup. It was _____.

2 The officer was not a lucky man. The officer was _____.

3 My fear of being buried alive was not rational. My fear was _____.

4 I was often in a deep, sleep-like state. I was often _____.

Vocabulary

6 Put the words into the correct categories below. Then add more words to each category.

> flu • a cold • a plaster • a bandage • a thermometer
> a pain killer • backache • heart disease • surgery • a fever
> medicine • an allergy • a jab • crutches • physiotherapy

MEDICAL PROBLEMS	FIRST AID EQUIPMENT	THERAPY

Grammar

7 Passives. Complete this newspaper article about a premature burial using the verbs in brackets.

Today, at the City Hall, an investigation into the death of Mrs. Legrange, wife of prominent lawyer Sidney Legrange, (**1**)_____ (start). It appears that the unfortunate lady (**2**)_____ (bury) alive some three years ago. Mrs. Legrange (**3**)_____ (put) into the family tomb three days after she (**4**)_____ (declare) dead. The investigators spoke to her husband and he said that the family tomb (**5**)_____ (open) on Tuesday for the burial of his aunt. He was horrified to discover that his wife had probably died in the tomb, not in her house as everyone had thought.

PRE-READING ACTIVITY

Speaking

8a The next story is called *A Descent into the Maelström*. It's about three sailors from Norway who are at sea when they are caught in a terrible storm. Work in pairs. How dangerous are these jobs? Rank them from 1 – 9 (9 is the most dangerous). Explain your reasons to each other.

1 ☐ miner
2 ☐ soldier
3 ☐ teacher
4 ☐ banker
5 ☐ sailor
6 ☐ police officer
7 ☐ doctor
8 ☐ farmer
9 ☐ fire-fighter

8b Now re-order the list again. This time imagine that it's a hundred years ago. Is your order now different?

Five

A Descent into the Maelström

We had now reached the highest part of the mountain. For some minutes, the man seemed too exhausted to speak. "Not long ago," he said, "I would have been a better guide. I would have been as fit as any of my three sons. But such a terrible thing happened to me.

"It was three years ago. Six hours of deadly terror have broken my body and my soul. You think I'm a very old man, but I'm not. In one day, my black hair went white and I became frightened, even of a shadow. I can't even look over the edge of this mountain."

To be honest, *I* was also terrified by the idea of looking over the edge of the mountain. We were, in fact, very high. I thought *he* was too close to the edge. It was windy and I was afraid that he would fall. I found it difficult to sit up and look into the distance in the wind.

"You must control your fears," said the guide. "I have brought you here so that you can have the best view of the event I was talking about.

"We are now," he continued, "near to the Norwegian coast. We are in the great province of Nordland. We are sitting on the peak of Helseggen, the Cloudy Mountain. Look. Below us you can see the sea. Sit up and look. If you feel dizzy, hold on to the grass. You won't fall."

I looked down and instantly felt dizzy. I could see the wide ocean and its ink-black waters. It would be difficult to imagine a lonelier or more deserted environment. To the right and to the left, as far as the eye could see, were dark cliffs and mountains. In the distance, there were a few deserted islands. The guide started to talk about the islands and the mountains. He told me their names and something about each one of them. Then, suddenly, he said, "Can you hear anything? Can you see any change in the water?"

I could. I could hear a loud sound and I could see that the sea was changing direction. It was a current[1]. Before my very eyes, this current became faster and faster. In five minutes, the whole sea, as far as the islands, was in torment. The waves were high. The sea was boiling, hissing, humming with whirlpools[2]. A few minutes later and the sea changed again. Now the surface was smooth and the whirlpools began to disappear. Then suddenly, without warning, they formed into one; one enormous whirlpool, about half a mile in diameter. In the center of the whirlpool was an enormous funnel[3]. It had an ink-black wall of water and it swirled[4] around faster, faster and even faster. At the same time, the noise it made was terrible. It almost screamed.

The mountain was shaking. I was shaking.

"This," said the old man, "is the Maelström. Boats, yachts and ships have been carried away by it. In 1645, the noise from it was so great that the houses in the port fell down. Sailors are afraid of this area of the sea."

I had read about the Maelström, of course, but nothing I had read had prepared me for this.

"Watch the whirlpool and while you are watching, listen to my story," said the guide. "I know more about the Maelström than any other man alive."

1. **current:** 水流
2. **whirlpools:** 漩渦

3. **funnel:** 漏斗
4. **swirled:** 打轉

I sat back in the shelter[1] of a rock to listen.

"My two brothers and I were fishermen, you know. We used to have our own boat. Most fishermen prefer the area to the south, despite the fact that here you get better fish. The only problem is that you have to be brave to fish around here. In fact, nobody was brave enough except us. We were always very careful to keep away from the area of the Maelström, although sometimes I got a bit nervous when the wind was strong. A sudden storm would be enough to put a fisherman in terrible danger. For six years, however, we did very well.

"Then, three years ago, there came a day which most people from this part of the world will never forget. We had the most terrible hurricane ever to come out of the sky.

"In the morning, the sky was blue and the wind was perfect for fishing. My brothers and I had no idea what was going to happen. We started at about two o'clock in the afternoon and by seven o'clock we were ready to go home. We had had a wonderful day. We had caught more fish than ever before. We were happy; the boat was full and there wasn't a cloud in the sky. We turned towards home. We had no idea of the danger ahead.

"When we were here, very close to Helseggen," the guide pointed his finger at the sea and the distant islands, "we were surprised when the wind changed direction. The wind was so bad and the current was so strong that the ship wasn't moving. Then, a large cloud developed in the sky. It was no ordinary cloud: this was a sandy red color. The wind died down. We had no way of moving. All we could do was sit there as the current took us along.

"In less than a minute, the storm arrived. Now it was so dark that

---

1. **shelter:** 這裏指保護

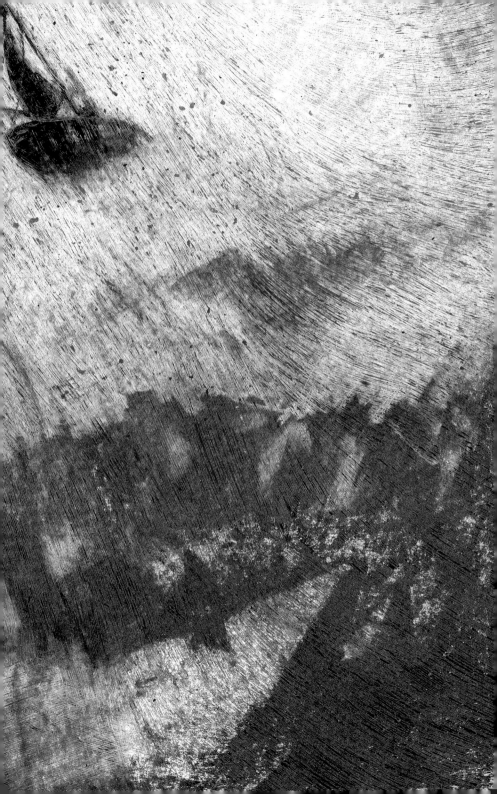

we couldn't see each other in the boat. I can't describe the force of the hurricane[1]. Even the oldest sailor in Norway has never experienced anything like it. Our masts[2] broke. I saw my youngest brother disappear into the sea. Of course, I never saw him again.

"I held on to a metal ring. The waves broke over my head. This seemed to go on for hours and hours, but it was probably only a few minutes. Then there was a break in the waves. I sat up and looked around me. My heart was filled with joy. My older brother! He was alive. My joy lasted for seconds before it turned into horror. I heard him scream 'Maelström!'.

"I started shaking. I thought my heart was going to burst. I couldn't hear him, but I understood from his lips what he was saying. There was nothing we could do. We were moving towards the Maelström and nothing could save us.

"By this time, the storm seemed to be over, although the waves were still enormous. The sky around us was still black, but directly above us the sky was blue; the bluest, brightest blue I have ever seen. We could see the moon; the fullest, brightest moon that I have ever seen.

"I looked at my brother. His face was pale. I screamed, but he couldn't hear me. He shook his head, 'listen!' he seemed to be saying. He knew. My brother knew that the Maelström was less than half a mile away. A wave, an enormous wave, took us high up into the sky. I closed my eyes in horror.

"The waves were smaller now. The sound had also changed. Before, there had been the sound of thunder, now there was a high scream. I knew we were about to enter the abyss.

"It may seem strange, but I felt quite calm. I began to think how

1. **hurricane:** 颶風

2. **masts:** 桅杆

magnificent it would be to die like a hero in the Maelström. I asked myself what it would be like – the inside of the whirlpool. I had been in a gale[1] many times before. A gale makes you blind and deaf. You can't breathe and it takes away all power of action. We had always been careful, we had always survived. This, however, was going to be the end. There was no way we could survive a descent into the Maelström.

"I'm not sure how long we were on the edge of the abyss, perhaps an hour. My brother was holding on to a barrel[2] which was tied to the side of the boat with ropes. As we got nearer to the funnel, he moved closer to me. He held on to the iron ring too. He realized that it wasn't big enough for both of us. I felt deep sadness when I realized his hands were trying to move mine. He wanted the ring for himself; he wanted me to die so that he could live for a few moments longer. I left the ring and, holding on to the remains of the mast, I moved to hold on to his barrel. I understood that he was mad with terror. I was doubly sad; neither of us had a chance of surviving the Maelström.

"Suddenly, we began to descend. I closed my eyes. It was sickening. I expected instant destruction. But moments passed and I was still alive. It took all my courage to open my eyes. I will never forget the sensations of wonder, horror and admiration I felt. The boat seemed to be hanging, as if by magic, inside the funnel. The funnel itself was enormous. It was deep, with perfectly smooth black sides. The moon was shining in a flood of golden glory along the black walls and down, down into the deepest parts of the abyss.

"We were swirling round. Round and round. At first, I was too afraid to observe the details. Then, helped by the moon, I looked down. I could see nothing except mist and the rainbow that lies between Time

1. gale: 強風   **2. barrel:** 桶子

and Eternity. We were traveling down, swinging and spinning in the whirl. Our progress downwards was slow.

"I began to see that we were not the only object caught in the Maelström. I could see ships and parts of ships, trees, parts of houses, furniture and boxes. It was strange how curiosity had taken the place of terror. I wonder which object will be the next to fall into the abyss, I thought. Perhaps that tree? I watched, with interest, as one thing after another suddenly stopped spinning, before it dropped deep into the funnel, lost forever.

"Then, I began to shake again. This time I was feeling something entirely different. Now I was feeling *hope*. I thought about the wood that we find on the shores. Perhaps some of it is thrown out of the Maelström.

"I noticed three things: the larger items fell fastest into the abyss, spherical items fell faster than those of irregular shape and cylinders were slower to fall than any others. I could see barrels above me. They were hardly moving downwards. They were just spinning around the wall of the funnel.

"I was thinking clearly, despite our desperate situation. We had one chance of escape. I cut some of the ropes from around my barrel. I tried to signal to my brother to do the same. He shook his head. He was determined to hold on to the iron ring. He was going to die on the ship, but I was going to try to save myself. I tied myself to the barrel and cut the last rope. Then, I did it; I jumped into the funnel.

"The result was as I expected. Success! I continued spinning around for about an hour, but I stayed at the same height. The cylinder shape of the barrel was helping me. Our ship, however, sank lower and lower.

I watched its progress in horror. Then its moment came; the ship suddenly dropped. Our ship, and with it my brother, dropped into the abyss.

"Moments later, the sides of the funnel became less steep and the whirl became less violent. The rainbow disappeared and the bottom of the funnel seemed to rise up. The sky was clear and the winds had gone down. Suddenly, I was on the surface of the ocean, above the spot where the Maelström had been and was no longer.

"I swam for a long time until I was picked up by a fishing boat. The fishermen were friends of mine, but they didn't recognize me: my hair was as white as it is today. Those six hours of terror in the Maelström had turned my hair from black to white. I told them my story, but they didn't believe me. Now I'm telling you and you probably won't believe me either."

Stop & Check

1 **Choose the best answer – A, B, C or D.**

1 The narrator is actually
   A younger than he seems ☐
   B older than he seems ☐
   C taller than he seems ☐
   D wiser than he seems ☐

2 The Maelström is
   A a type of current in the sea ☐
   B a port on the coast of Norway ☐
   C a type of storm ☐
   D an enormous whirlpool ☐

3 The guide is telling the story of events that happened
   A in 1645 ☐
   B six hours before ☐
   C when he was a child ☐
   D three years before ☐

4 When he was caught in the Maelström, the guide had been fishing
   A with his two brothers ☐
   B with his two sons ☐
   C with his two friends ☐
   D with his father ☐

5 The guide tied himself to a barrel
   A because he wanted to stay on the ship and experience the fall into the abyss ☐
   B because his brother had suggested it ☐
   C because he couldn't stand up on the boat ☐
   D because he noticed that cylinders didn't fall into the abyss ☐

6 When he came out of the Maelström, the guide was
   A picked up by a fishing boat ☐
   B picked up by friends who were looking for him ☐
   C able to climb onto an empty boat ☐
   D able to swim to the shore ☐

Vocabulary

2 Write the relevant adjective for each of these geometrical shapes under its diagram.

cylinder • square • triangle • rectangle • sphere • oval

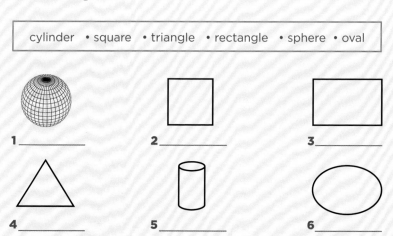

1_____

2_____

3_____

4_____

5_____

6_____

3 Choose the weather words from the box which best complete the sentences below.

• lightning (n) • boiling (adj) • breeze (n) • hurricane (n) • freezing (adj) • icy (adj)

1 There was a nice _____ by the sea, so the temperatures were very pleasant.

2 It's _____ outside – take your gloves with you.

3 That tree was struck by _____ last week.

4 Be careful. The roads are _____ after last night's frost.

5 I was wearing a T-shirt, but I was still _____.

6 The _____ is getting nearer to the Florida coast.

Grammar for First

4 Use the word given in capitals at the end of some of the lines to form a word that fits in the gap **in the same line**.

Hurricanes

Hurricanes, cyclones and typhoons are (**1**)_____ **DESTROY**
forces of nature. The (**2**)_____ rain and very **TORRENT**
high winds (**3**)_____ with hurricanes cause **ASSOCIATION**
flooding and can damage trees and buildings. In
the Northern Hemisphere, air spirals anticlockwise
to cause a hurricane, (**4**)_____ the Southern **LIKE**
Hemisphere, where it spirals clockwise. The
eye of the storm can be more than 300 km in
(**5**)_____, but the hurricane is much more **WIDE**
dangerous as the eye gets (**6**)_____. When this **NARROW**
happens, the wind speed increases (**7**)_____. **VIOLENT**
Today, a large number of meteorologists monitor
hurricanes as they develop. Satellite images are
very (**8**)_____ in tracking the progress of **USE**
hurricanes so that people are prepared for them.

Writing

5 Summary Writing. Write a short summary of events in *A Descent into the Maelström*. Include the connectors below in your summary.

- although
- in spite of
- however

Speaking

6 **Work in pairs. Discuss your answers to the questions below.**

1 Have you ever done any water sports?
2 Is there a water sport that you would like to try?
3 Which of the following sports are the most dangerous? Why?
  • scuba diving
  • water skiing
  • powerboat racing
  • platform diving
4 In general, do you prefer holidays by the sea or holidays in the mountains? Why?
5 What do you think we should do to protect our beaches and seas?

PRE-READING ACTIVITY

Listening

7 **Listen to the first part of the next story, *The Murders in the Rue Morgue*. Choose the best answer - A, B or C.**

1 What does the narrator say about Dupin?
  A He has an analytical mind. ☐
  B He lives in Lyon. ☐
  C He likes sport. ☐
2 Residents in the area were woken up by
  A the police. ☐
  B screaming. ☐
  C loud music. ☐
3 The door on the fourth floor was
  A open. ☐
  B locked. ☐
  C broken down. ☐
4 The mother's body was found
  A in the garden. ☐
  B in the fireplace. ☐
  C in the street. ☐

Six

The Murders in the Rue Morgue

▶ 6 A few years ago, I was living in Paris in a comfortable old house in the Faubourg St. Germain. I shared the house with Monsieur C. Auguste Dupin. He was a young man, very well-read, with the sort of analytical mind I have always admired. He went on to become one of the greatest criminal investigators. His first criminal case[1] was the Murders in the Rue Morgue and this is the story of how he solved it.

One morning, we were sitting in the study, reading the newspaper, when the following story caught our attention.

EXTRAORDINARY MURDERS

This morning, at about 3 a.m., people who live in the Quartier St. Roch were woken up by the sound of a woman's screams. The screams came from a house in the Rue Morgue where a certain Madame L'Espanaye lived with her daughter, Mademoiselle Camille L'Espanaye. A group of neighbors and two *gendarmes*[2] broke down the front door. By this time, the screams had stopped, but they could hear two voices arguing upstairs. The neighbors and the *gendarmes* ran up the stairs, but when they arrived at the second

1. **case:** 案件   2. **gendarmes:** 法國憲兵

floor, everything was perfectly quiet. They searched every room on the second floor and every room on the third floor. Eventually, they arrived at a large room on the fourth floor. The door was locked and the key was on the inside, so the *gendarmes* broke down the door.

Inside, the room was very untidy. The furniture was broken and overturned. On a chair, there was a razor, covered in blood. In the fireplace, there were some grey human hairs, also covered in blood. On the floor, there were some coins, an earring, three large silver spoons and two bags containing nearly four thousand francs[1] in gold. Mademoiselle L'Espanaye's body was in the fireplace. There were deep scratches on her face and throat. She had been strangled[2]. Her mother, Madame L'Espanaye was not to be seen.

The *gendarmes* searched the rest of the house and Madame L'Espanaye's body was finally found in the garden, at the back of the house. Her throat had been cut.

***

7   The next day, the newspaper had more information – an interesting introduction to the main witnesses in the murder case.

WITNESSES TO THE TRAGEDY IN THE RUE MORGUE

The Paris police interviewed the witnesses in this tragic case. Here is a summary of what they know:

1. francs: 法郎   2. strangled: 勒死

Pierre Moreau, shopkeeper. He has known the two women for about four years. They had been living in the house for about six years. He says that the two women lived a very quiet life and didn't have many visitors.

Isidore Musèt, *gendarme*. He says that he was called to the house at about three o'clock in the morning and that he found a group of neighbors trying to get in through the street door. He could hear screaming coming from one of the upstairs rooms. The screams stopped and then they heard a loud argument. There were two voices: one was a man and the other was a very strange voice. The witness then described the state of the room.

The neighbors. They were unsure about the voices. They agreed that one was definitely a man and he was definitely French. The second could have been either a man or a woman. They were unsure whether the second person was Italian, German, English, Russian or another nationality. The room was locked from the inside and it was perfectly silent when they reached it. The windows were closed and locked from the inside, too. The chimney was too small to allow any human being to climb up it.

Adolphe le Bon, bank clerk. He said that Madame L'Espanaye had some property. She often visited the bank. Three days before her death, she had taken four thousand francs out of the bank.

Paul Dumas, doctor. The doctor described the terrible injuries on the two bodies. He was certain that a woman would not be strong enough to kill them. Mademoiselle L'Espanaye had been strangled. Her mother's throat had been cut, probably with the razor. Both the women had broken bones and terrible bruises[1].

★★★

Dupin was very interested in the case. He asked for my opinion. All I could do was agree with the rest of Paris; it was a mystery and it would probably never be solved.

"There is one problem," said Dupin. "The Paris police are very careful and they work very hard, but there is no *method* in their work. I think we should look at these murders ourselves. It will be interesting to see the scene of the crime. I know the Prefect of Police, we can easily get permission."

The following day, Dupin got permission and we went immediately to the Rue Morgue. Before we went inside, Dupin examined the street, the neighboring buildings and the rear of the house itself. We then went into the house and into the room where Mademoiselle L'Espanaye's body had been found. Dupin looked carefully at everything.

Then, we left. Dupin said nothing until lunchtime the following day. "Did you notice anything *peculiar* at the scene of the crime?" he asked.

"No, nothing *peculiar*," I replied.

"People think the crime will never be solved because there seems to be no motive: no motive for the violence of the crime, no motive for the untidiness of the room. *I*, on the other hand, have solved the mystery. It is very simple indeed."

---

1. **bruises:** 瘀傷

I stared at Dupin in astonishment.

"I am now waiting for a person to arrive," he continued. "That person is not the killer, but he is partly responsible. He may not come, but I think he probably will. We will need to arrest him, so here is a gun."

Dupin continued, "We must apply *method*[1]. It can't be a murder followed by a suicide. Madame L'Espanaye was not strong. Her own broken bones and terrible bruises mean suicide is impossible. Therefore, we have murder. This murder has been committed by another person, or persons."

"Go on," I said.

"Now we come to the voices. All the witnesses agree that the first voice belongs to a man and that he is a Frenchman. The *peculiar* thing is that the witnesses disagree about the second person. It can't be a woman, because of the victims' terrible injuries. They can't decide if he is an Italian, a German, an Englishman or a Russian. This means they think that he's a foreigner. However, all this really means is that they didn't understand him.

"Now, let's consider the room. How did they escape from the locked room? The chimney is too small. There was a large crowd in the street, so they didn't escape from the front windows. The murderers *must* then have escaped through the back windows."

"But the windows were locked," I said.

"Apparently so, but I applied *method*. The back windows were the only possible means of escape. I checked the locks. One window was indeed locked. The other window was difficult to reach, because the bed was in front of it. It certainly *looked* locked. The police were satisfied with this. *I*, on the other hand, was not. I tried to open the window. The

1. **method:** 條理

lock was broken and the window opened easily. When I closed it again, it still had the *appearance* of being locked. Therefore, the murderer, or murderers, escaped through the back windows."

"But how did they get down from the fourth floor? It's impossible."

"You have made the same mistake as the police. It *looks* impossible. But there are shutters[1] on the windows and the shutters were partly open. Someone could climb down from shutter to shutter, although that person would have to be extremely agile[2]. So we have someone extremely agile, with a very strange voice, speaking a very strange language that no-one can understand."

I had no ideas.

"Now we come to the hairs. Some grey hairs were found by the fireplace. I also found some other different hairs in the same place. Look at them."

"But they aren't human!" I exclaimed.

"I agree. Now, read this."

Dupin passed me an encyclopedia. It was open at "O". I read a description of an orangutan[3]. I read about their enormous strength and their great agility and I began to understand the horrors of this murder.

"This morning," Dupin went on, "I placed an advertisement in the newspaper. I said that an orangutan had been found. I am expecting the first man, the Frenchman the neighbors heard, to come to collect his animal."

The doorbell rang. "Come in!" said Dupin. "Come in and tell us all about the murders in the Rue Morgue!"

The man saw our guns. He knew he was caught, so he told his story. He was a sailor and the owner of the orangutan. When he was not

---

1. **shutters:** 護窗板
2. **agile:** 靈敏

3. **orangutan:** 紅毛猩猩

at sea, he lived quietly in his apartment and his orangutan had never caused any trouble. None of his neighbors knew about the animal, because he didn't know any of his neighbors. The day of the murders, the sailor had been shaving in his apartment, when the animal had picked up his razor and run out into the street. The sailor had followed him through the neighborhood as far as the back of the Rue Morgue, but the orangutan had been enjoying his taste of freedom. There, the orangutan had climbed up the L'Espanaye women's building and in through the open window on the fourth floor. He could hear the terrible screams and, being a sailor, our man had no difficulty using the shutters to climb up behind the orangutan. When he got to the window, the orangutan had already killed the daughter. The poor animal had probably been frightened by the woman's screams. Our man, the sailor, shouted at the orangutan, telling him to stop, but the animal attacked the old lady with the razor. Hearing the neighbors shouting, the animal was afraid, dropped the razor and threw the old lady's body out of the window. The animal then escaped through the window, which closed behind him and he disappeared into the back gardens of the Rue Morgue. The sailor was afraid and ran away.

★★★

Naturally, we took the sailor to the Prefect of Police. He was happy that the murders had been solved, although he was less happy that Dupin, with *method*, had solved the case. The police decided that the sailor was innocent. He eventually recaptured his orangutan, after searching all over Paris for him.

And the orangutan? It now lives with other monkeys in the zoo in the Jardin des Plantes.

Stop & Check

1 **Are the statements true (T) or false (F)? Correct the false statements.**

T F

1 Auguste Dupin is a professional police officer. ☐ ☐
_____
_____

2 Dupin and the narrator got most of their facts about the ☐ ☐
murders from newspaper reports.
_____
_____

3 The old woman's body was found in the fireplace. ☐ ☐
_____
_____

4 The murderers had stolen the old woman's money. ☐ ☐
_____
_____

5 An orangutan was the real killer of the two women. ☐ ☐
_____
_____

6 The sailor never saw the orangutan again. ☐ ☐
_____
_____

2 **Who am I? Write the character's job next to the description.**

1 I live in Paris. I share a house with another person and I have an analytical mind. I'm very interested in mysteries: I believe that people can solve mysteries by applying reason. _____.

2 I travel a lot in my job. When I am not working, I stay at my apartment in Paris. I don't really know anyone in Paris and no-one really knows me. _____.

3 I often saw Madame L'Espanaye. The last time I saw her was three days before her death. _____.

4 I'm an important person in Paris. I'm the head of the police force. _____.

Wordsearch

3 **There are nine adjectives from *The Murders in the Rue Morgue* in this wordsearch. Find them and put them into the gaps in the sentences below.**

1 The room was very q*uiet* . (5 letters)

2 He was a young man with the sort of a_____ mind I have always admired. (10 letters)

3 The Paris police interviewed the witnesses in this t_____ case. (6 letters)

4 The doctor was certain that a woman would not be s_____ enough to kill them. (6 letters)

5 It will be i_____ to see the scene of the crime. (11 letters)

6 "Did you notice anything p_____ at the scene of the crime?" he asked. (8 letters)

7 "That person is not the killer, but he is partly r_____." (11 letters)

8 "But how did they get down from the fourth floor? It's i_____." (10 letters)

9 The police decided that the sailor was i_____. (8 letters)

I	P	E	P	E	C	U	L	I	A	R
A	N	A	L	Y	T	I	C	A	L	I
C	I	T	H	A	V	M	O	R	J	N
Q	U	I	E	T	L	P	Y	F	X	N
S	I	X	C	R	T	O	D	A	E	O
T	R	A	V	E	E	S	A	V	L	C
R	E	S	P	O	N	S	I	B	L	E
O	O	E	K	C	E	I	T	T	E	N
N	U	W	R	E	L	B	G	I	R	T
G	S	U	N	D	T	L	A	R	N	X
T	R	A	G	I	C	E	L	A	Y	G

Writing for First

4 **This is part of a letter from an English-speaking friend.**

We've just finished reading The Murders in the Rue Morgue *in class and I know you've read it, too. What did you think of it? Did you like the ending? Have you read any other detective stories?*

Write a letter to your friend giving your opinion.

Write 120-180 words.

Grammar for First

5 **Use of English. Complete the second sentence so that it has a similar meaning to the first sentence, using the word given. Do not change the word given. You must use between two and five words, including the word given.**

1 The room needed searching well.

have

You ought _____ well.

2 Check the windows as they might not have been locked.

case

Check the windows _____ locked.

3 "Why don't we look in the back garden?" Dupin asked.

suggested

Dupin _____ in the back garden.

4 Dupin never panics about his work.

control

Dupin _____ his work.

5 "I'd prefer to start the search immediately," said the Prefect.

rather

The prefect said _____ the search immediately.

Vocabulary

6 **Phrasal Verbs. Complete these sentences in a logical way. Use your dictionary to double-check the meanings of the phrasal verbs.**

1 He **picked up** the newspaper and _____.
2 "**Look out!**" said the man. "There's _____!"
3 They decided to **put off** the visit because _____.
4 She was too tired to **carry on**, so she decided _____.
5 They **checked up** on his alibi and _____.
6 Applications for the job came **flooding in** because _____.
7 I **ran into** my neighbor by the cinema. He was _____.
8 Dupin **found out** that _____.

PRE-READING ACTIVITY

Speaking

7 **The name of the next story is _The Stolen Letter_. Work in pairs to answer the questionnaire.**

1 When was the last time you wrote a letter?
  a recently
  b I've never written a letter
  c other: _____

2 How much does it cost to send a normal-sized letter in your country?
  a I don't know
  b I never buy stamps
  c It costs _____

3 How often do you text?
  a three times a day
  b once a week
  c _____

4 What type of letter do you think was stolen in the story? Say why.
  a a love letter
  b a letter to a pen-friend
  c a letter from a diplomat in a foreign country

Seven

The Stolen Letter

(Original title: The Purloined Letter)

In Paris, one autumn evening, I was sitting in my study, reading. My friend, Monsieur C. Auguste Dupin, was with me. He was also reading and we hadn't spoken for at least two hours. We were interrupted by the doorbell and in came the Prefect of the Parisian Police.

"Come in!" said Dupin, smiling. "We haven't seen you for a long time! Not since the murders in the Rue Morgue."

The Prefect was a little embarrassed at the mention of the famous murders: the police prefer not to talk to amateurs[1], especially when the amateur in question has solved a case. "I've come to ask your opinion about a case," he said.

"What's the problem?" asked Dupin. "I hope it isn't another murder."

"No, no. It's probably something very simple. I'm sure my police officers will have no problems with it, but I thought you would be interested. It's such a very peculiar thing."

"Simple and peculiar," said Dupin. "Interesting. If it's *simple*, then the police should have no problems at all."

"Hmm," said the Prefect. "Let me tell you. But first, I must tell you that secrecy is of great importance in this case. I would probably lose my job if anyone found out that I have told you."

---

1. amateurs: 業餘人士

"Your secret is safe with us," I said, and Dupin agreed.

"Good," continued the Prefect. "A very important letter has been stolen from the royal apartments. We know who took it; he was seen taking it. We know that he still has the letter."

"How do you know?" asked Dupin.

"Because nothing has happened yet."

"I don't understand," I said.

"Because, the information in the letter is very important. If the person who has the letter made the information public, there would be a scandal[1]. The honor of this important person would be at risk.

"The thief is a Minister. We shall call him Minister D. The theft was very clever indeed."

The Prefect of Police paused, for effect, and then went on, "It's like this. The very important person receives the letter while she's alone in the royal office. While she's reading the letter, her husband comes into the room. She wants to hide the letter from him, but there's no time. She puts the letter on a table. Only the address is visible and her husband doesn't notice. At this point, Minister D comes into the room. He immediately sees the letter, recognizes the handwriting and notices that the lady is afraid. He talks about business for a few minutes. Then he gets one of his *own* letters from his pocket and puts his letter on the table *next* to the lady's letter. He carries on talking for a few minutes, then he picks up the *lady's* letter from the table. He puts *her* letter into his pocket and leaves the room, leaving his own letter on the table. The lady sees this, but can't say anything because her husband is in the room."

"Very clever. Has the Minister used the information in the letter to his own advantage?" asked Dupin.

---

1. scandal: 醜聞

"Oh, yes. The information is being used. Minister D is now a very powerful man in politics. He is blackmailing[1] her. He is able to influence events in a very dangerous way. The lady is desperate. She has asked me to get the letter back."

"It is clear," said I, "that the Minister still has the letter. When he makes the letter public, he will lose his power."

"I know," said the Prefect. "I've searched his apartment. I have, of course, searched it *in secret*. He mustn't know that we suspect him. Fortunately, he hardly ever stays at his home in Paris and he doesn't have many servants. I have keys, you know, that can open any door in Paris. For the last three months, I personally have spent every night searching his house."

"Perhaps he has hidden the letter somewhere else," I suggested.

"No, he must keep it near him at all times. He must be ready to produce the letter at a moment's notice. The letter is definitely at his home. He doesn't keep it with him, either. I've sent the two best street thieves in Paris to search him. They couldn't find anything."

"Tell us about your search of his house," I said.

"We searched the whole house, room by room. We opened every possible drawer and we checked that there weren't any secret drawers. Then we inspected the chairs and all the cushions. We removed the tops from all the tables to check inside the table legs. We used a powerful microscope to examine every piece of furniture. We checked the mirrors, the paintings, the beds, the carpets and the curtains. When we had finished, we began to check the structure of the house.

"We searched every square centimeter of the place and the two houses next to it. We even examined the gardens."

---

1. **blackmailing:** 威脅

"You've certainly taken a lot of trouble," I said.

"It's a very important case. There must be no scandal and, of course, there is a large reward."

"Did you look through all the Minister's papers?" asked Dupin.

"Yes. And through all the books in his library – page by page. We have looked everywhere."

"Then perhaps you are wrong and the letter is not in D's house," I said.

"Perhaps you're right," said the Prefect. "What do you suggest, Dupin?"

"I imagine that you have a very good description of the letter, so you know exactly what you are looking for. I'm sure you have given all your officers a very good description of it. I suggest you search the house again," he replied.

"There's no point!"

"Then I have no other suggestion to make," Dupin replied.

***

A month later, the Prefect came to visit us again. "I did as you suggested, Dupin, but I still can't find the letter."

"How much is the reward?" asked Dupin.

"I can't say, I'm afraid. But *I* would give fifty thousand francs to anyone who found the letter for me," replied the Prefect. "The case is now extremely urgent and the reward has been doubled."

"In that case, write me a check for fifty thousand francs, now. When you have signed it, I will give you the letter."

I was astonished. The Prefect was astonished. He pulled his check book out of his pocket. He paused, looked at Dupin and then wrote a check for fifty thousand francs. He gave the check to Dupin, who looked carefully at it, then put it into his pocket. We both stared as Dupin then walked over to his desk, unlocked a drawer and took out a letter. He gave the letter to the Prefect. The Prefect's face was a picture of joy and delight. He opened the letter, quickly glanced[1] at its contents and ran out of the room and out of the house, without saying a single word.

When he had gone, my friend began to explain. "The Parisian police work very hard. I knew that the search of Minister D's house would be as complete as possible, however, I knew that their search would be limited. It was limited because they were only looking in the places where they *themselves* would have hidden the letter. They assumed that all people would hide a letter in a chair leg or inside a curtain. The Minister is not a fool. I know him and he is actually a poet and a mathematician. He has imagination and a calculating mind. The Minister knew perfectly well that his home would be searched. He deliberately stayed away from his house in Paris so that the police *could* search it! I became certain that the Minister had not hidden the letter at all.

"I made my plan. I ordered a pair of dark glasses and called, one fine morning, at his house. The Minister was at home and invited me inside. He pretended to be relaxing on the sofa, although he is the most energetic man I know. I apologized for the dark glasses, telling him I had some problems with my eyes. Of course, he couldn't see my eyes, so I was able to look around the room without him knowing.

1. **glanced:** 偷看

84

"There was a desk near his sofa with a few letters on it, but they weren't what I was looking for. It didn't take me long, however, to find the one I *was* looking for.

"I glanced at a small letter rack[1] near the fireplace. In it were some invitations and a single letter. The letter was old and torn, almost in two. It looked as if someone had been disturbed when they were throwing it away. I asked the Minister a question about a topic of great interest to him and while he was talking and talking, I studied the letter from my chair. Then I said goodbye to the Minister and went out of the room, leaving my gold pen on the table.

"The next morning, I went back to the Minister's house for my pen. While we were talking, there was the sound of a shot from the street, followed by screaming. D ran to the window and opened it to look out. I quickly took the letter from the letter rack and replaced it with a copy. I had spent the previous night making a perfect copy of the letter, the letter I had studied in the Minister's apartment."

"You were lucky that the Minister was distracted by the sound of the shot in the street," I commented.

"Lucky?" said Dupin. "The shot in the street came, of course, from a man I had paid. There was no danger to anyone and my man was able to escape."

"Why did you put a copy of the letter into the letter rack?" I asked.

"For my own protection," said Dupin. "D could have seen me by the letter rack. And also because the lady will now have control over the Minister. The Minister doesn't know that he doesn't have the letter. He will continue to blackmail her and she can decide when to end his career. This is a horrible crime. I would like to see his face

1. **letter rack:** 信架

when he opens my copy of the letter."

"Why? Did you write something inside?"

"Of course, it seemed a shame to leave it blank. Also, Minister D once behaved very badly towards me when we were in Vienna. The opportunity was too good to miss. These are the words I copied –

Such a horrible plan, if it's not worthy of Atreus, it's certainly worthy of Thyestes.

"Explain," I groaned, confused.

"It's a classic story of revenge. I am Atreus, I stole his letter and that was wrong, but this is my revenge. Minister D is Thyestes and he committed the original crime. Here, have a look at this."

Dupin threw a large book at me. "Read the story. All intelligent men need to know their Greek myths!"

Stop & Check

1 **Put these nine events from *The Stolen Letter* into chronological order.**

1 ☐ The lady asks the Prefect of Police to find her letter.

2 ☐ Dupin returns to the Minister's house and substitutes the letter with a copy.

3 ☑ A very important person receives a private letter and she doesn't want her husband to know about it.

4 ☐ Dupin visits the Minister and sees the letter.

5 ☐ The Prefect is delighted when Dupin gives him the letter.

6 ☐ He uses it to blackmail the lady.

7 ☐ Therefore, the Prefect of Police searches the Minister's home, but doesn't find the letter.

8 ☐ The Prefect is desperate, so comes to Dupin for help.

9 ☐ Then, Minister D steals the letter from the very important person.

Vocabulary

2 **Which of these words is the odd one out? Write your reason underneath.**

1 ☐ steal   ☐ rob   ☐ burgle   ☐ give

2 ☐ simple   ☐ easy   ☐ complex   ☐ uncomplicated

3 ☐ find   ☐ search   ☐ investigate   ☐ examine

4 ☐ astonished   ☐ surprised   ☐ amazed   ☐ disappointed

5 ☐ table   ☐ chair   ☐ desk   ☐ cushion

Speaking for First

3 **Exchanging Opinions. Work in pairs. Discuss the questions below. Use prompts from the box to help you.**

stating opinions	asking for opinions
In my opinion, In my view, I think ... I'm not sure if ...	What do you think? Have you got a view? Do you think that ...?

1 Do you watch thrillers or detective stories on TV?

2 Why do you think so many people enjoy this type of TV programme?

3 Do you think there is too much emphasis on crime on the TV news and in newspapers?

4 What other types of TV programme do you enjoy?

5 What about the future, do you think our TV viewing habits will change? How?

Grammar

4 **Verbs and Prepositions. Complete each sentence with a verb from the box and a preposition. Make sure the verb is in the correct form.**

> • congratulate • depend • prevent • pay • blame
> • succeed • belong • look

1 We'd all like to *congratulate* you *on* winning the gold medal.

2 They _____ him _____ losing the keys.

3 This book _____ _____ the public library.

4 The goalkeeper's job is to _____ the other team _____ scoring a goal.

5 My sunglasses! I've been _____ _____ them everywhere.

6 I'd like a holiday, but it _____ _____ how much money I can save.

7 She finally _____ _____ passing that horrible exam.

8 I had to stand in line for hours just to _____ _____ the coffees.

Grammar

5a **Conditionals. Put the verb in capitals into the correct form to complete the sentences.**

1 I'll get the later train if _____ .
MISS

2 If the Minister had hidden the letter, the Prefect _____ .
FIND

3 If I were you, I_____ the time of your flight.
CHECK

4 Dupin would have found the letter, if he _____ the Minister's house.
SEARCH

5 I _____ a new phone, if I had enough money.
BUY

6 He won't understand unless you _____ it to him.
EXPLAIN

7 If the mechanics had found the problem, our car _____ .
NOT BREAK DOWN

8 You wouldn't feel so tired, if you _____ to bed earlier.
GO

5b **Talk in pairs. Discuss what you would do in the following situations.**

- If I had the time ...
- If I had the patience ...
- If I had the money ...

Vocabulary

6 **Put these actions into chronological order.**

☐ Stick the stamp on
☐ Get a reply
☐ Seal the envelope
[7] Write a letter
☐ Wait for a reply
☐ Write the address on the front
☐ Buy a stamp
☐ Put it in an envelope
☐ Post the letter

7 **Three-part Phrasal Verbs. Match the verb to the correct dictionary definition then complete the sentences with the correct verb, in the right form.**

1 look up to   ☐ **a)** accept something bad, patiently

2 make up for   ☐ **b)** feel happy that something is going to happen

3 look forward to   ☐ **c)** admire someone, respect someone

4 put up with   ☐ **d)** do something good to put right something less good

1 It's important for children to have a role model they can _____.

2 I bought you this to _____ missing your party.

3 I'm really _____ the holidays.

4 I'm leaving. I can't _____ this any longer.

PRE-READING ACTIVITY

Writing

8 **The next story is *Ligeia*: a story of love, death and obsession. The first line is in the box below. Continue the story from your own imagination.**

> *I cannot, for my life, remember how, when or even exactly where, I first met the lady Ligeia.*

Now read Poe's story and compare it with your own.

Eight

Ligeia

8 I cannot, for my life, remember how, when or even exactly where, I first met the lady Ligeia. Long years have passed for sure, and my memory is weak from suffering. Perhaps the learning, the unusual beauty and the low musical voice of the woman I loved made their way into my heart gradually. Perhaps that's why I don't remember.

I think I first met her in some large, old city on the Rhine. She talked about her family – it was an ancient one, I'm sure.

Oh, Ligeia! Ligeia! I can see the image of she who is no more.

And now, while I write, I realize that I never knew, and have never known, the paternal name of my friend, my love, my wife. Was it Ligeia's game? Was it her intention that I should never ask about her father and her family? Was she testing the strength of my love? Or was it *my* decision – was it my own romantic idea never to ask about her family?

My memory will never fail me on the subject of the *person* of Ligeia. She was tall and quite slim and, as she got older, she could even be called painfully thin. She was majestic, yet her footstep was light. She came and went like a shadow. I was never aware of her when she came into my study, until I heard the sweet music of her voice, or felt her cold hand on my shoulder. She was the most beautiful woman I have ever seen. Yet her features were not classically beautiful. There was a strangeness in her face. Her skin was pure, and her hair! Her hair was raven-black[1]. Shiny and naturally curly, her hair was beautiful.

I could use hundreds of references from Hebrew, Greek and Roman literature to describe Ligeia, except for her eyes. We have no models from the ancients. Her eyes were larger than usual. They were full and blacker than black, with the same color echoed in her eyelashes. The strangeness of her eyes was in their expression.

I have thought about Ligeia's eyes for many years. Ligeia's character has also been the object of my study for many years. She was intense in thought, in action and in speech. Although she seemed calm and controlled, Ligeia was passionate about everything. She had a fierce[2] energy and this was all transmitted through her delightful, yet terrifying, eyes. It was also transmitted through her calm, low voice which was so in contrast with the wild words she often used.

Ligeia's learning was very wide. She was excellent at classical languages as well as modern European tongues. She was a scientist too, and a philosopher, and a mathematician. Her learning was incredible and she loved to study.

Without Ligeia, I was like a small, lost child. Her voice made our studies pure pleasure but, as the years passed, I began to notice a difference. Her eyes shone less upon the page. Ligeia became sick and her eyes became wilder. Her pale fingers began to look like fingers from the grave. I realized that Ligeia was going to die. It was hard for me to go on, knowing that she was going to die, but I realized

---

1. raven-black: 烏黑光亮   **2. fierce:** 猛烈

that Ligeia was fighting too. She was fighting to live, with a passion and energy I had not expected. I had thought she would face death calmly, without terror. Not so. Her resistance to the Shadow was fierce. I wanted to help her, but it was impossible to calm that wild desire to live.

I never doubted that she loved me; but I should have known that her love would be deep and passionate. For hours and hours she talked to me about her love for me, and her devotion to me. I didn't deserve such love. It was incredibly deep. How terrible it was to hear about it, just at the point when she was about to leave me.

At midnight of the night she died, she made me read a poem she had written. As I read its last words "Out – out are the lights – out all!", I heard a terrible scream.

"Oh God!" cried Ligeia, jumping to her feet. "Why must I die like this? Why must I die? Save me!"

She fell, exhausted with emotion, back onto her Death bed. She breathed her last. Ligeia had died.

***

I couldn't stand the lonely desolation of my house on the Rhine any more. I had been wealthy already and Ligeia had brought me even more riches. I left Germany and, after a few months of traveling around Europe, I settled in England. I bought and restored an abbey in one of the wildest, loneliest areas of the country. The building was gloomy. In my sorrow, I spent my days filling the house with incredible things. I bought gorgeous furniture and fabulous carpets and gold tapestries. I adored my house and everything in it.

Then, in a moment of extreme madness, I married the fair-haired, blue-eyed Lady Rowena Trevanion of Tremaine.

Rowena's family were proud people. I was surprised that they had allowed their daughter to marry a man like me. But then, they had a thirst for gold – and gold was something I had plenty of.

If I describe my wife's bedroom, you will see how mad I had become. The room was in one of the towers of the abbey. It was shaped like a pentagon and in one wall there was an enormous window. The window was made of glass from Venice, and the color was so grey that the rays of the sun or the moon gave the room a ghostly light. The ceiling was high and decorated with Gothic scenes. The room was lit with the light of a hundred candles and an enormous chandelier[1]. There were statues from Greece and Egypt, heavy gold curtains at the windows and around the bed. There was gold thread everywhere. The effect was terrible – the room was a triumph and it was almost alive.

It was clear, from the first month of our marriage, that my new wife didn't love me and had married me for my money. She was, however, afraid of my bad temper. This gave me some satisfaction, because I actually hated her. My memory flew back to Ligeia, the lovely, the intelligent, the beautiful, the dead Ligeia. I remembered her purity, her wisdom, her passion. In my madness, I would call out her name at night. Ligeia! Surely she could not have left me for all eternity!

At the beginning of the second month of our marriage, the Lady Rowena became sick. She had a fever and was sleeping badly. She spoke of strange sounds in her room and strange movements behind the tapestries and in the curtains. I told her it was undoubtedly her

1. chandelier: 吊燈

imagination. She got better. Then, a short time later, she became even more violently sick. The doctors had no idea what the problem was, but I noticed that she was afraid. Again, she talked about the curtains and tapestries moving unexpectedly and strange sounds, in and around her room.

One night, near the end of September, she talked to me again about her fears. She had just woken up. I had been sitting near her bed, watching, half-anxious and half-terrified. Her body was now painfully thin. She was clearly very sick indeed. She talked about the sounds *she* could hear that *I* couldn't hear. Her face was pale with terror. I went to get her some water, but as I walked across the room, I saw a shadow, the shadow of some sort of being on the rich golden carpet underneath the chandelier. What was it? Was it an angel? Or was it an evil being? I said nothing and gave Rowena the water. As she raised the glass, I saw or *thought* I saw, three or four large drops of blood-red liquid fall into the glass. Rowena hadn't seen the drops fall. Had I? Had I dreamt it? I wasn't sure. My wife drank the water. As soon as she had drunk it, there was a rapid change in her condition. She was now even closer to the hour of her death.

I sat in her room for three days and three nights. On the third night, she died.

★★★

The servants prepared her body for the tomb. They covered her with a shroud and they covered her hair with a scarf. I did what husbands do when their young wives die; I sat with my dead wife in her room.

I stared at the painfully thin body in the shroud and at the scarf that covered her blonde hair. I was filled with horror at Lady Rowena's sudden death, but all I could think about was Ligeia. A thousand memories rushed back into my heart. I stayed there, as tradition demanded, staring at my second wife, but thinking about my first.

About midnight, although it could have been earlier, I heard a groan. It was the cry of a woman. The noise was coming from the bed of Death. I listened again, but there were no more sounds. I stared at the bed, but Rowena's body was not moving. Was it my imagination? There was no repetition of the sound, but I had to keep staring at Rowena's body. I couldn't take my eyes off her. A few minutes later, I was aware of a change of color in her face. I was horrified. Rowena was alive! I thought about calling the servants, but they were in another part of the abbey and I didn't want to leave her. A moment later and the color had faded from her cheeks. She looked even paler and icier in death than she had before. Again, I returned to thoughts of Ligeia.

An hour later, I was again aware of some sound coming from the bed. Horrified, I rushed over and saw that her lips were moving. Then, the lips relaxed and I could see Rowena's small white teeth. I was amazed. She was alive. I put every effort into restoring life fully; I held her hands, I shook her shoulders. Hope faded again as the color left her face and she was a dead body once more.

Again, I thought about Ligeia and again, I heard the groan from the bed. This drama of death and life was repeated and repeated and repeated until morning. Each time that my second wife returned to death, I thought of my first, Ligeia. Each time

Rowena returned to death, she seemed icier and chillier even than before.

Then, as the first rays of ghostly light came through the window, my wife got slowly up from her bed. She really was alive! I sat in terror, as she walked hesitantly into the center of the room and stood under the chandelier. She was standing in the place where I had seen the shadow. I stared in fascination, horror and dread. My brain was paralyzed. How could this be possible? Could this be the living Rowena in front of me? Could this be Rowena at all – the blue-eyed, fair-haired Lady Rowena Trevanion of Tremaine? Why? Why should I doubt it? *But how could she have grown taller?*

Mad with hope and fear, I ran over to her. She took off her scarf and there it was, there was the stream of long, black, raven-black hair; it was blacker than midnight! And now the eyes opened.

I knew. I couldn't believe my eyes. "I cannot be mistaken!" I cried out. "These are the eyes, the full black, wild eyes of my lost love – of the lady – of the LADY LIGEIA!"

Stop & Check

1 **In these sentences, which of his wives is the narrator describing?**
A Ligeia
B Rowena

Write A or B in the box.

- ☐ "Shiny and naturally curly, her hair was beautiful."
- ☐ "Her face was pale with terror."
- ☐ "Her learning was incredible and she loved to study."
- ☐ "Her resistance to the Shadow was fierce."
- ☐ "She came and went like a shadow."
- ☐ "She had married me for my money."
- ☐ "She was majestic, yet her footstep was light."
- ☐ "She was tall and quite slim."
- ☐ "She was, however, afraid of my bad temper."
- ☐ "The fair-haired, blue-eyed lady."

Vocabulary

2a **Match the phrasal verbs with their synonyms.**

1 to prepare	**a** ☐ to go back
2 to meet	**b** ☐ to settle down
3 to fail someone	**c** ☐ to get to
4 to go to live	**d** ☐ to let someone down
5 to return	**e** ☐ to get ready
6 to arrive	**f** ☐ to run into

2b **Now put the correct phrasal verb into the context sentence. Be careful with the verb form.**

1 It's getting late. It's time we _____ home.
2 I _____ him at the market yesterday. I hadn't seen him for ages.
3 I'm sorry about this. I feel I've _____ everyone _____.
4 They've decided to move to Seattle. They want to _____ there.
5 It was nearly midnight by the time we _____ the airport.
6 I'd like to _____ dinner _____ now.

Grammar for First

3 Read this history of the ghost story. Decide which answer (A, B, C or D) best fits each gap.

Ghost Stories

(**1**)_____ history, people of all cultures have enjoyed telling and listening to ghost stories. There are examples of ghost stories from (**2**)_____ Egypt and from Greek, Roman, Arabic and Indian literature. Many critics (**3**)_____ that the most important writer of this type of story was, in fact, the Irish writer, Sheridan Le Fanu. His work and that of American author, Edgar Allan Poe, made ghost stories extremely popular in the nineteenth century. Of course, with the (**4**)_____ of film in the twentieth century, ghost stories reached an even greater (**5**)_____.
In the early days, there were both good and bad ghosts and many of the films were quite sentimental, until the horror genre became popular and there was a decline in the traditional ghost story. Today, (**6**)_____, many people enjoy watching the large number of reality television programmes involving ghost-hunting and contact with the dead. Typically, these programmes visit famous haunted places, especially at times like Halloween, and try to document (**7**)_____ there really are ghosts there. Of course, ghost stories don't have to relate to one person; there are stories of ghost animals, armies, ships and many other (**8**)_____. Spooky!

1 A ☐ All	**B** ☐ By	**C** ☐ From	**D** ☐ Throughout
2 A ☐ ancient	**B** ☐ old	**C** ☐ elderly	**D** ☐ past
3 A ☐ tell	**B** ☐ argue	**C** ☐ want	**D** ☐ told
4 A ☐ advent	**B** ☐ history	**C** ☐ start	**D** ☐ arrive
5 A ☐ people	**B** ☐ audience	**C** ☐ readers	**D** ☐ cinemagoers
6 A ☐ actually	**B** ☐ since	**C** ☐ although	**D** ☐ however
7 A ☐ whether	**B** ☐ because	**C** ☐ often	**D** ☐ factually
8 A ☐ types	**B** ☐ meanings	**C** ☐ people	**D** ☐ reasons

Speaking

4 **Talk in pairs. Discuss your answers to the questions below.**

- Do you read ghost stories? Why do/don't you like them?
- Do you ever tell ghost stories to your friends?
- What other types of fiction do you read?
- Do you read non-fiction?
- Have you ever read an e-book?
- How important is it for children to read a lot?
- How important are illustrations in a book?

Speaking for First

5 **Work in pairs. Follow the instructions below. When you are comparing the pictures, try to use some of the phrases from the box. While your partner is comparing the pictures, count the number of adjectives s/he uses.**

- In the first picture ... while in the second ...
- In the first picture ... whereas in the second ...
- Both pictures show ...
- In one of the pictures ...

Student A Look at the pictures on p 73 and p 85. Both pictures show people holding paper. Compare the pictures and say why you think they are holding the paper. Talk for about a minute.

Student B Look at the pictures on p 97 and p 111. Both pictures show people looking out of a window. Compare the pictures and say why you think they are looking out of the window. Talk for about a minute.

Grammar

6 Might. Rewrite the sentences, using the correct form of the word *might*.

1 It is possible that the film is a thriller.
The film _____.
2 I'm not sure whether I will go to the party.
I _____.
3 Perhaps he got caught in traffic.
He _____.
4 I will possibly go out on Saturday.
I _____.
5 They probably won't have time.
They _____.
6 I don't know if she has bought a new computer.
She _____.

PRE-READING ACTIVITY

Listening

▶ 9 **7a The next story is called *The Fall of the House of Usher*. Listen to the first part of the story and tick the adjectives you hear.**

- ☐ dull
- ☐ soundless
- ☐ cheerful
- ☐ gloomy
- ☐ desolate
- ☐ delightful
- ☐ depressing
- ☐ beautiful
- ☐ dead
- ☐ glorious
- ☐ dying
- ☐ dreadful

7b What do the adjectives you have ticked have in common?

Nine

The Fall of the House of Usher

9 For a whole, dull, dark, soundless, autumn day, I had been traveling alone, on horseback, through the countryside. It was almost evening when I reached the House of Usher. As soon as I saw it, my heart was filled with a sense of total gloom. I looked at the scene in front of me. I looked at the house. I saw its sad, lonely walls and its vacant windows. The garden was the same – depressing – just a few dying trees, a dead hedge[1] and a black lake. There was an iciness in my heart, although I couldn't explain why. What was it? Why was the House of Usher so dreadful? Perhaps some places are just depressing.

I got off my horse by the black lake. I looked at the reflection of the trees, the house and the vacant, eye-like windows. I thought about the reason for my visit. I was planning to stay in this house of gloom for a few weeks. Roderick Usher had been my childhood friend, although I hadn't seen him for many years. I had recently received a strange letter from him. Roderick had seemed sick and depressed, he wrote about his wish to see me again. I was surprised to hear from him, but agreed to visit him anyhow.

I didn't really know very much about Roderick Usher. My friend had always been shy, but then his family had been famous for its shyness.

1. **hedge:** 樹籬

There had been many great artists in the Usher family and sensitive musicians, too. They had always given money to charity, but in a quiet, constructive way. The family was known as the House of Usher, because the title had always passed from father to his only son, over the centuries. No brothers or cousins had ever inherited the house; it had only ever passed to the son.

I looked down into the silent lake, which made me feel even more depressed. There was something almost supernatural about the atmosphere here. The air was foul[1]. I looked more closely at the ancient house. The whole building was covered in fungus. The individual stones were falling to pieces, but the house was still standing. However, there was one crack in the front of the house. It went from the roof to the ground, but it was very narrow. I rode over a small bridge to the doorway. A servant took my horse and into the House of Usher I went – through the Gothic doorway.

Another servant led me on a long journey through dark, silent corridors to his master's study. The journey did nothing to change my first, negative impression. The black floors, the dark pictures and the armor[2] on the walls made me feel even worse. Roderick's study was large with a very high ceiling. The windows were long, narrow and pointed, but very little light came through them. The room was full of antique furniture and even the books and musical instruments in the room failed to make it look comfortable. There was an air of deep gloom.

Usher stood up when I came in. He was obviously very pleased to see me. We sat down. I have never in my life seen a man as changed as Roderick Usher. He had been pale and fair as a boy, but now his skin

---

1. **foul:** 邪惡的   2. **armor:** 盔甲

was ghostly pale. His eyes were extraordinarily large and watery and his hair? Well, his fair hair was now pale, thin and very, very long. He was clearly very nervous.

Roderick Usher explained his reasons for inviting me. He was sick, he said. It was a family sickness and he was unlikely to get better – it was a nervous condition. He couldn't eat, because food was too salty. He could only wear certain fabrics next to his skin. He couldn't stand the smell of flowers. Even a little bit of light was too bright for him and all sounds were unbearable, except that of his guitar.

"I will die like this," he said. "I must die in this condition. I know all about terror and I know I must fight against one terrible thing – FEAR."

There was more. He hadn't left his house for many years and he knew that the gloom of the house, garden and lake had had an effect on his mind. But the greatest reason for his depression was the terrible and long-lasting sickness of Madeline, his sister.

"She has been my only companion for many years and she is my last relative on this earth. When she dies, I will be the last of the ancient House of Usher," he said to me one day.

While he was speaking, Madeline walked into the room and straight out through another door, without noticing that I was there. I was astonished and I was, although I couldn't explain why, terrified. I looked at her brother, but he was holding his head in his hands. "She is close to death," he said, in tears. "You will never see her again."

For the next few days, Roderick and I spent our time reading and painting. Sometimes I also listened to the poetry of his guitar. I wanted to help my friend to overcome his fear and depression. He talked and talked about his feelings and I began to realize that I could do nothing to help him through the darkness and gloom. He didn't mention Madeline once.

In many ways, Roderick was mad. His paintings described the darkness of his mind in a way that words could never do. One of his abstract paintings comes to mind. It was a small picture showing the inside of a long, rectangular tunnel with low, smooth, white walls. It was clearly a tunnel into the darkness of the earth. There was no obvious light in the picture, but the whole painting was bathed[1] in a ghostly splendor. His music was also uncontrolled and he sometimes wrote wild words to go with his pieces. One song I remember was called 'The Haunted Palace'. It was a strange song about happiness lost. After he had sung it, Roderick talked for a long time about his family home. He talked about the old stones, the fungus, the dying hedge and trees and the black lake. He talked about the armor and the long history of his family and how it was closely connected to the house. Roderick clearly thought his present condition was caused by his family history and by the house itself.

As well as music and conversation, we also read a lot. The books we read and enjoyed were Roderick's old favorites. I wasn't sure, however, that his choice of reading helped his mental condition; he loved mystical, spiritual stories and stories of heroism. He read about ancient religions and mysterious dreams.

One evening, we were reading in his study, as usual. Roderick seemed worried. Without warning, he suddenly told me that Madeline had died. He also said that he was planning to keep her body for two weeks in one of the cellars[2] in the house, before she was finally placed in the family tomb. I was surprised at this, but I helped him place

1. **bathed:** 披光

2. **cellars:** 地下室

Madeline's body in its coffin and take it down to the cellar.

The cellar was small and damp. There was no window, so the room was totally dark. The cellar also happened to be directly under my room. In the past, the cellar had clearly been used as a prison cell, so it had a large, heavy door. The door made the terrible sound of metal on metal as it moved.

We put the coffin down and looked at Madeline for the last time. I was shocked at the similarity between the sister and brother. Usher understood. He told me that they had been twins and that they had always understood each other perfectly. Madeline's face was still slightly pink and there was a suggestion of a smile on her lips – so terrible in death. We put the lid on the coffin and returned upstairs. I noticed that the upstairs rooms were almost as gloomy as the cellar.

Roderick Usher was terribly sad and bitter. He couldn't read, paint or play his guitar. He walked around the house, from room to room. He seemed even paler now, although how was that possible? His voice had also changed; it was now high and shaky, perhaps with terror. It almost seemed to me that his mind was tortured by some terrible secret and that he didn't have the courage to talk about it. Sometimes he sat for hours in silence. His condition terrified me and even began to have an effect on me. I began to be influenced by his wild imagination.

I experienced the full power of this, his wild imagination, on the seventh or eighth night after we'd put Madeline's coffin into the cellar. I couldn't sleep. The hours passed and still I couldn't sleep. I could just see the outlines of the gloomy furniture in my room. The curtains were moving gently in the wind. What was that noise? There was a storm outside, but there was another low sound I could just hear. I sat up, in total alarm, and stared into the darkness. I got dressed and went out into the corridor.

"Have you seen it?" he said. "You must see it! The lake is glowing[1]."

He ran to the windows and threw them open. The strength of the wind almost knocked us over. It was a stormy, yet beautiful night. But everything, everything around us – the house, the garden and the lake – was glowing in unnatural light. There was a supernatural, foul air.

"Close the windows!" I shouted. "This air is dangerous, you are sick! What you can see has a simple explanation," I shouted. "What you can see is just a trick of the light, it's an electrical storm."

I had to do something, but what? I tried to catch Roderick's attention. "Look, here's one of your favorite books. I'll read it and you can listen."

He was as pale as usual, but now there was an air of panic about him. I picked up the nearest boo k. It was a novel about knights and dragons. It was a ridiculous story, but I read aloud and Roderick seemed to listen.

"Sir Ethelred rode furiously into the forest," I read. "Where was the Black Knight? He felt the wind and rain against his face and there, in the darkness, there was the castle. He rode up to its great wooden door, but the door was locked. Ethelred started to break down the door. There was a terrible noise as the wood cracked and the door broke open."

At the end of this sentence, I stopped. I could hear it, in a far part of the House of Usher. Was it from the cellar? I could hear the exact same sound; the sound of wood cracking. I hoped Roderick hadn't noticed. I continued the story: "The good knight, Ethelred, broke down the door and entered the castle. He looked around quickly. The floor and walls were made of silver. He found no sign of the Black Knight. Instead, in

1. **glowing:** 發光

front of him, there was a dragon. On the wall, behind the dragon, there was an enormous gold plate with the words:

If you are here, a good knight you must be

Now kill the dragon and your lady will be free!

"Ethelred attacked the dragon with his sword. The dragon breathed fire, but he was no match for the good knight. The dragon let out a terrifying scream – it was so horrible and so…"

Here, I was interrupted again. I heard it. I really did. I heard a scream, a terrifying scream, just like the one described by the novelist. Again, it seemed to come from the cellar. Had Roderick noticed these sounds? He seemed to be half asleep. I didn't want him to get any more nervous, so quickly, I continued reading the story: "Ethelred climbed over the dragon's body and took the gold plate from the wall. It was so heavy that the knight dropped it. The noise it made as it fell on the silver floor was tremendous."

No sooner had I spoken these words, than I heard the same sound of metal on metal from the cellar. I jumped up to my feet in a state of absolute panic. This time I was certain. "Roderick! Did you hear that?"

I ran over to my friend. I shook his shoulders. His face was like stone and his eyes were staring into the distance. "Roderick! Did you hear that noise?"

"Hear it? Did I hear it? Yes, of course I heard it," he groaned. "I hear it all the time; for hours, for days I've heard it. She is alive! She was alive when we put her into her coffin and she's alive now. Remember that terrible smile on her lips? Remember the pink of her cheeks? The same night, the night after we put her into the cellar, I heard her scratching at the wood. She was scratching at the wood of her coffin, desperate to escape. I heard that many days ago. I didn't dare speak, I didn't dare say anything to you."

He paused. His voice was high and his nervous exhaustion was obvious. "And now, tonight," he went on. "Ethelred, the good knight? Ha. Ha," he laughed. "It wasn't the knight you heard, was it? There was no sound of Ethelred breaking down the door. What we actually heard was the wood of her coffin finally breaking. Then we heard the noise of metal on metal as she broke down that heavy door. Then we heard her screaming. There is no escape. She will be here in no time at all. I can hear her footsteps on the stairs. Can you hear it too? I can hear the beating of her heart. Fool!" he cried.

Roderick jumped to his feet and pointed at the heavy wooden door. "There is nowhere, nowhere I can hide! Nowhere I can take shelter! She's standing outside this room now!"

At that moment, the door opened, as if some superhuman energy had been needed to push it open. It was only the power of the wind, but Roderick was right. There, outside the door, she stood. There, indeed, stood the tall, painfully thin figure of the lady Madeline of Usher. There was blood on her white shroud, evidence of a terrible fight. For a moment, she stood shaking by the door. Then she fell in the violent agony of death onto her brother. They both fell to the floor, she was dying and he was already dead, killed by the terrors he had been afraid of.

I ran. I ran and ran. I ran from that room and I ran from that house. The wind was still strong and the storm was still violent, as I ran across the bridge and through the hedge. Suddenly, a wild light shot along the path in front of me and I turned to see where it might have come from. The enormous house and its dark shadows were behind me. The light was the light from a full blood-red moon, enormous as it went down behind the house. I stood for a moment, bathed in its terrible light.

Then I saw the crack in the front of the house, the crack I had noticed when I first arrived. I stared, in terror; the crack was getting wider. I stared and stared as the crack got even wider. Then, I saw it. Starting from the crack, I saw the enormous walls come down. There was a long, shouting sound, like the voice of a thousand waters. The deep dark lake closed silently over the stones of the House of Usher.

Stop & Check

1 **Answer the questions about** *The Fall of the House of Usher.*
Support your answers with evidence from the text.

1 What makes the narrator go to visit Roderick Usher?

2 What is the narrator's first impression of the house and gardens?

3 How does the narrator describe Roderick's appearance?

4 What do we learn about Madeline Usher before she is put into her coffin?

5 What is unusual about Roderick Usher's paintings?

6 How much do we know about Roderick's state of mind before his death?

7 What has Roderick been able to hear since Madeline was put in the cellar?

8 What happens to the Usher family home at the end?

Grammar for First

2 **Use the word given in capitals at the end of some of the lines to form a word that fits in the gap in the same line.**

Gothic Fiction

The *Fall of the House of Usher* is an example of a genre of fiction which was very popular in the **(1)**_____ century – Gothic. This type of fiction was often **(2)**_____ and also often had elements of horror in it. The first stories of Gothic fiction **(3)**_____ in the century before and they were inspired by medieval traditions and **(4)**_____. Some of the greatest novels in the English language, **(5)**_____ *Frankenstein, Dracula, Northanger Abbey, The Turn of the Screw* and *The Strange Case of Dr Jekyll and Mr Hyde*, are part of the genre. **(6)**_____, Gothic themes are used in other media, such as film and music, too.

NINETEEN

ROMANCE

ORIGIN

ARCHITECT
INCLUDE

NATURAL

Vocabulary

3 **Adjective Crossword. Use the clues below to complete the crossword with words from _The Fall of the House of Usher_.**

Clues Across

1 Very frightening indeed. t_____ (10 letters)
3 Dark and depressing, like the house. g_____ (6 letters)
6 Not well, not healthy. s_____ (4 letters)
7 Mysterious, almost religious. m_____ (8 letters)
8 An opposite of bright. d_____ (4 letters)
9 "Now his skin was g_____ pale." (7 letters)

Clues Down

2 Very, very large. e_____ (8 letters)
4 There were just a few d_____ trees in the garden. (8 letters)
5 "I began to be influenced by his w_____ imagination." (4 letters)
6 Not noisy, very quiet. s_____ (6 letters)

Edgar Allan Poe (1809 – 1849)

Edgar Allan Poe is one of the most important American writers of short stories. He also wrote poetry and was a literary critic. Although he was famous in his lifetime, he found it difficult to earn a living as a professional writer. He was sick in the later part of his life and died at the age of only forty.

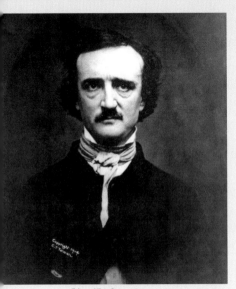

Edgar Allan Poe

Virginia Clemm

Early Life

Edgar Poe was born on January 19, 1809, in Boston, Massachusetts. His parents were both professional actors. His mother and father died before he was three years old and, after that, he went to live with John and Frances Allan. His name was changed to Edgar *Allan* Poe, although the couple did not adopt him. He was an intelligent boy and was given an excellent education. For five years, from 1815 to 1820, Edgar's family lived in Scotland and London and he went to school there.

Family Life

Poe started university in Virginia, but left after the first semester. He had debts, which caused problems for him with the Allans. In 1827, when he was eighteen years old, he joined the army in an attempt to be independent. He also published his first book of poems in the same year.

In 1829, Frances Allan died and John Allan and he were reconciled for a short time. When Allan remarried, the following year, they argued again. In 1831, Poe decided to leave the army. He moved from city to city, earning his living by writing critical reviews and articles for journals and newspapers. Poe married his cousin, Virginia Clemm, when he was 26 years old. The marriage was at first a secret, as Virginia was thirteen years old at the time.

Writing

It was particularly difficult to be a professional writer in the early nineteenth century. Poe was often paid very little for short stories and articles in magazines, so he continued working as a journalist and reviewer. He also had a number of patrons, who helped him financially. This enabled him to continue to write poetry. One poem, *The Raven*, was an overnight success. He published it in 1845, but he was still not very rich.

Although he is famous as a writer of Gothic romantic fiction, Poe is often credited with being the first author of detective stories and the creator of the "locked room mystery" (a common device in detective fiction). Arthur Conan Doyle, the creator of Sherlock Holmes, said that Poe's work had had a great influence on him. Poe was also a writer of science fiction and made a contribution to the development of this genre.

Later Years

Edgar Allan Poe's later life was a battle with sickness. His wife, Virginia, died in 1847 and life became very difficult for Poe after that. He died two years after his wife, in 1849. The cause of his death was a mystery: various reports give various reasons for his death but it remains a mystery today.

Gustave Doré, *The Raven*

Task

Complete the form with the information about Edgar Allan Poe.

Name: _____

Date of Birth: _____

Place of Birth: _____

Genres of Writing: _____

Most Famous Poem: _____

Name of Wife: _____

Date of Death: _____

Genre, Themes and Symbols

Genre

In his writing, Poe experimented with many different genres of short story. He wrote several historical stories such as *The Masque of the Red Death* and *The Pit and The Pendulum*. This was a common thread in Gothic fiction. Poe was not always careful about making sure that his historical details were correct. An example of this comes from *The Pit and the Pendulum*: by the time the French army entered Toledo, the Spanish Inquisition was not as violent as it had been earlier. This makes the story less believable. Besides historical and detective fiction, Poe was also interested in exploring science fiction: *A Descent into the Maelström* is an example of this, as is his novel *The Narrative of Arthur Gordon Pym of Nantucket*. However, Poe is probably best known for his Gothic fiction.

Death

Death is obviously one of Poe's recurring themes. *Ligeia* is often cited as symbolizing the death of the most important women in Poe's life - his mother, foster-mother and his young wife. Death is a common theme in Gothic fiction, as is burial or the fear of being buried alive. This type of fiction was particularly popular in the early nineteenth century, so Poe may have been writing to please his audience.

Eyes

Eyes are a recurring symbol in Poe's work. In *The Tell-Tale Heart*, the old man's eye is the key to his murder. Similarly, in *Ligeia*, her dark eyes, contrasted with the blue eyes of the narrator's second wife, are an indication of Ligeia's power. Roderick Usher has very prominent, watery eyes in *The Fall of the House of Usher*.

Illustration for Edgar Allan Poe's story "Ligeia" by Harry Clarke (1889-1931), published in 1919

Light, Darkness and Color

Color is also important in Gothic fiction. Perhaps *The Masque of the Red Death* is the most obvious example of this in Poe's work. Not only is there the symbolism in the black room with the ebony clock, there are also frequent references to scarlet and the color of blood. Shadow and the play of light and dark are also important in most of the stories in this collection.

The Clock and Time

We find frequent references to time in Poe's short stories. In *The Tell-Tale Heart*, the beating of the old man's heart is compared to the ticking of a clock. In *The Masque of the Red Death*, the ebony clock controls the dancing and music at the Masquerade Ball and, in *The Pit and the Pendulum*, the figure of Time seems to control the pendulum.

Task

Think about the stories in this collection and answer the questions

1 Color is important in other stories besides *The Masque of the Red Death*. Which ones?

2 Write a paragraph about Poe's use of light and darkness.

3 Critics talk about Poe's use of the 'double' or *doppelganger*. Think about this with reference to *The Fall of the House of Usher*.

Great Detectives in Fiction

C. Auguste Dupin, Edgar Allan Poe's creation, is considered by many to be the first detective in this genre of fiction, although there are examples from older Chinese and Arabic literature. Today, there are many different types of detective in crime fiction: police officers, amateurs, judges, journalists, private eyes, lawyers, forensic scientists, priests and even animals.

Sherlock Holmes

Created by Arthur Conan Doyle, Sherlock Holmes is probably the most famous detective. He is an amateur, not a professional, and is often accompanied by his friend and narrator Dr Watson. Holmes is similar to Dupin, in that he relies on logic and rational thought to solve mysteries.

Hercule Poirot

Another amateur detective is Agatha Christie's creation, the Belgian, Hercule Poirot. In the tradition of Sherlock Holmes and C. Auguste Dupin, Poirot is a believer in using 'the little grey cells' (brain cells) to solve mysteries.

Commissaire Maigret

Maigret, created by Georges Simenon, is an example of a police detective. Poe and Christie's eccentric detectives are seen as more intelligent than the police - Maigret is, however, a brilliant, ordinary policeman. Popular all over the world, the Maigret novels have been made into TV series and films in many countries.

Philip Marlowe

Raymond Chandler created Philip Marlowe, a tough private investigator. He's a very different kind of detective from those above - he's more of an action man. He's still a thinker, but the stories have a lot more action in them.

Modern Detectives

Modern crime thrillers are as popular as those from the 'Golden Age'. They are all very different, too. Crime solvers such as Blomqvist and Salander from *The Girl with the Dragon Tattoo* use investigative journalism and computer hacking and deal with modern social problems. Andrea Camilleri's Inspector Montalbano is concerned with contemporary social and political issues. Henning Mankell's Wallander is a dark, introspective personality, very different from the more two-dimensional characters in earlier detective fiction.

Task

Choose two fictional characters from the list below (or from two different crime writers you have read) and do some Internet research. Write a paragraph comparing the two detectives.

Robert Langdon
Father Brown
Lisbeth Salander
Salvo Montalbano
Jane Marple
Sam Spade

Andrea Camilleri's Inspector Montalbano

Meteorology

In *The Fall of the House of Usher*, Roderick and the narrator are both aware of a strange glow in the sky and around the lake. Light and weather conditions could cause such similar effects.

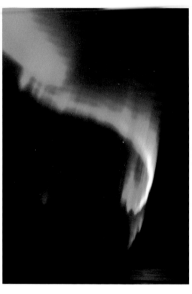

Rainbows

We all know about the colors we see in a rainbow. Can you remember why they happen? First of all, you can't see a rainbow unless the sun is shining behind you. There also needs to be humidity in front of you. We see rainbows when the light of the sun is refracted through a drop of rain (or lots of drops of rain): see diagram.

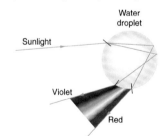

This causes the light to be split into its different colors. It's a scientific phenomenon.

There probably isn't a pot of gold at the end of the rainbow, actually, there isn't even an end! Rainbows are part of a circle - we just don't always see the whole circle, unless we're in an airplane.

aurora borealis

Perhaps the strange glow in *The Fall of the House of Usher* could have been caused by *aurora borealis*. This strange phenomenon is seen in the sky near the North and South Poles. Near the North Pole, it's called *aurora borealis*, meaning the Northern Dawn. Most people call it the Northern Lights. Near the South Pole, the effect is very similar and its name is *aurora australis*, or Southern Lights. It happens when charged particles are attracted by the magnetic poles. Colored light is radiated when they strike gas particles in the atmosphere. The colors from the *aurora* range from yellow and green to red and blue.

Mirage

A mirage is another trick of the light. Although they are associated with deserts, you can even see a mirage on a road on a hot day. Your eye thinks it sees water, but there isn't any. Why does this happen? Just like with a rainbow, light is refracted from warmer air towards cooler air. Because the air near the road is hotter than the air in the sky, light rays seem to hit the eye from a different place. This causes it to look like there is water on the road - or in the desert - in front of you, when there isn't.

Fog or Smog

Perhaps the ground was particularly warm in the area around the House of Usher. If that were the case, then maybe the glow was actually fog. If there were no clouds in the sky, the ground would radiate heat. That would cause it to cool very quickly when it hit the air and form water vapor - fog - near the ground. If it were in a smoky, industrial area, the water vapor could mix with particles from smoke and form smog.

Task

Internet research

Have a look on the Internet. Find out more about smog. What are its causes and what are its effects? Write a paragraph about it.

TEST YOURSELF 自測

1 **Answer the questions about these *Stories of Mystery and Suspense*.**

1 Do you think the narrator in *The Tell-Tale Heart* is mad? Why?

2 What does the clock symbolize in *The Masque of the Red Death*?

3 Describe the prison cell in *The Pit and the Pendulum*.

4 In *The Premature Burial*, what is the narrator's greatest fear?

5 According to the text of *A Descent into the Maelström*, what exactly is the Maelström?

6 What is Dupin's criticism of the Paris police in *The Murders in the Rue Morgue*?

7 Why does Dupin return to the Minister's apartment in *The Stolen Letter*?

8 How does the narrator feel about his second wife in *Ligeia*?

9 What happens to Madeline in *The Fall of the House of Usher*?

2 **Find a word in English for these definitions. The words are all from the glossary.**

1 To make a low sound when you are in pain

2 To have the courage to do something

3 Darkness

4 Able to move very well and very easily

5 To ask someone for money because you know something bad about them

6 To shine or be light when everything is dark

SYLLABUS 語法重點和學習主題

Verbs:
tenses with *This is the first* ...,
Present Perfect Continuous,
Past Perfect Continuous,
perfect infinitives,
Future Perfect,
a wide variety of phrasal verbs,
complex passive forms,
wish/if only

Types of Clause:
type-three conditionals,
mixed conditionals,
relative: embedded, defining

Modal Verbs:
might, may

Answer Key 答案

//

Stories of Mystery and Suspense

Pages 6-7

1   1A 2B 3A 4D 5C 6B 7D

2   **2** scream - screamed **3** reply - replied **4** answer - answered **5** exclaim - exclaimed
6 cry - cried **7** shout - shouted **8** whisper - whispered

3   Various possible answers.

Pages 16-19

1   **1** T
2 F - He had never had problems with the old man.
3 F - The narrator went to look at the old man.
4 F - He was awake.
5 T
6 F - He could hear the sound of the old man's heartbeat.

2a sharpness-sharp bravery-brave fury-furious care/carefulness-careful wisdom-wise evil-evil
dullness-dull cleverness-clever

2b **1** wise **2** evil **3** careful **4** furious

3   **1** was the first time
2 wish you could have seen
3 asked whether he had slept
4 take as long
5 I were you I would

4   Various possible answers.

5a Possible answers:
1 You wear a watch, a clock is on the wall.
2 You usually groan if you are in pain and you scream if you are angry or frightened.
3 You have four fingers and one thumb on each hand.
4 A lantern is a type of light.
5 A shadow is the shape an object makes when light is behind it. Shade is when you are not in
the sun.
6 You need a bell to ring. You can use your hand to knock on a door.

5b **1** watch **2** shade **3** lantern
6a Various possible answers.
6b **1** T **2** T **3** F **4** T **5** F **6** T

Pages 28-31

1   Possible answers:
1 He and friends were going to lock themselves away in the abbey.
2 Because it was on a steep hill with high walls and nobody from outside could get into it.
3 He had organized lots of food, entertainers, musicians, ballet dancers and clowns.
4 Each one was decorated in a different colour.
5 The music stopped and people stood still.
6 Midnight/Twelve o'clock.
7 Because the stranger was wearing a Red Death costume.
8 The clock stopped and the torches and lanterns went out.

2a 1 c 2 e 3 f 4 a 5 b 6 d

2b 1 time is money

    2 have made good time

    3 from time to time

    4 to kill time

3   Various possible answers.

4   Various possible answers.

5 1 which/that 2 in/during 3 between 4 as 5 less 6 During 7 in 8 When 9 to 10 was

6a 1 c 2 f 3 d 4 a 5 b 6 e

6b Various possible answers.

7   Various possible answers.

Pages 40-43

1   5-8-9-4-1-2-6-7-3

2a homicide - murderer - to muder/to kill

    theft - thief - to steal

    fraud - fraudster - to defraud

    blackmail - blackmailer - to blackmail

    arson - arsonist - to set fire to

    rape - rapist - to rape

    shoplifting - shoplifter - to shoplift

    burglary - burglar - to burgle/burglarize

    robbery - robber - to rob

2b Various possible answers.

3   1A - 2C - 3B - 4D - 5A

4a 1 e 2 f 3 d 4 c 5 a 6 b

4b 1 tick/clang 2 splash 3 hum 4 clanging

4c Various possible answers.

5 1 Although 2 In spite of 3 however

    1 In the 12th century 2 1478 3 auto-da-fé

    4 Because they were Spanish territories 5 In the 19th century

6a 1 c 2 h 3 f 4 e 5 g 6 b 7 d 8 a

6b Various possible answers.

Pages 52-55

1   a C b D c A d B e C f B g A h A i C j D k C l A

2   1 terrible 2 alive 3 diseases 4 in the meantime 5 respected 6 stiff

3   Various possible answers.

4   1 of 2 without 3 although 4 to/with 5 by

    6 such 7 by 8 from 9 an 10 due

5a 2 unable 3 irrelevant 4 illogical 5 unfortunate 6 inedible 7 irregular 8 illiterate

    9 unconscious 10 impatient

5b 1 inedible 2 unfortunate 3 irrational 4 unconscous

6   MEDICAL PROBLEMS

    flu a cold backache heart disease a fever an allergy

    FIRST AID EQUIPMENT

    a plaster a bandage a thermometer crutches

    THERAPY

    a painkiller surgery medicine a jab physiotherapy

7   1 started 2 was buried 3 was put 4 was declared 5 was opened

8   Various answers possible.

Pages 64-67

1 1A 2D 3D 4A 5D 6A

2 1 shperical 2 square 3 rectangular 4 triangular 5 cylindrical 6 oval

3 1 breeze 2 freezing 3 lightning 4 icy 5 boiling 6 hurricane

4 1 destructive 2 torrential 3 associated 4 unlike 5 width 6 narrower 7 violently 8 useful

5 Various answers possible.

6 Various answers possible.

7 1A 2B 3B 4A

Pages 76-79

1 1 F - He's an amateur detective.

2 T

3 F - Her body was found in the garden. Her daughter's body was found in the fireplace.

4 F - They hadn't stolen anything.

5 T

6 F - He found the orangutan.

2 1 Detective 2 Sailor 3 Bank clerk 4 Prefect of police

3 2 analytical 3 tragic 4 strong 5 interesting 6 peculiar 7 responsible
8 impossible 9 innocent

I	P	E	P	E	C	U	L	I	A	R
A	N	A	L	Y	T	I	C	A	L	I
C	I	T	H	A	V	M	O	R	J	N
Q	U	I	E	T	L	P	Y	F	X	N
S	I	X	C	R	T	O	D	A	E	O
T	R	A	V	E	E	S	A	V	L	C
R	E	S	P	O	N	S	I	B	L	E
O	O	E	K	C	E	I	T	T	E	N
N	U	W	R	E	L	B	G	I	R	T
G	S	U	N	D	T	L	A	R	N	X
T	R	A	G	I	C	E	L	A	Y	G

4 Various answers possible.
5 **1** have searched the room
    2 in case they were not
    3 suggested (that) we looked
    4 is always in control of
    5 he would rather start
6 Various answers possible.
7 Various answers possible.

Pages 88-91
1 3-9-6-1-7-8-4-2-5
2 Possible answers:
    1 give - the others all mean to take away
    2 complex - because it means difficult
    3 find - the others all mean to look for
    4 disappointed - it always has a negative meaning
    5 cushion - it is soft furninshing, not furniture
3 Various answers possible.
4 **2** *blamed* him *for* **3** *belongs to* **4** *prevent* the other team *from* **5** *looking for*
    6 *depends on* **7** *succeeded in* **8** *pay for*
5a Possible answers:
    1 I miss the early one **2** would have found it **3** would check **4** had searched
    5 would buy **6** explain **7** would not have broken down **8** went
5b Various answers possible.
6 Possible order:
    6-9-3-1-8-4-5-2-7
7 4-3-1-2

    1 look up to **2** make up for **3** looking forward to **4** put up with
8 Various answers possible.

Pages 100-103
1 **1** "Shiny and naturally ... = A
    2 "Her face was ... = B

3 "Her learning was ... = A
4 "Her resistance to ... = A
5 "She came and went ... = A
6 "She married me ... = B
7 "She was majestic ... = A
8 "She was tall ... = A
9 "She was, however ... = B
10 "The fair-haired ... = B

2a 1 e 2 f 3 d 4 b 5 a 6 c

2b 1 went back 2 ran into 3 let (everyone) down 4 settle down 5 got to 6 get (dinner) ready

3 1D 2A 3B 4A 5B 6D 7A 8A

4 Various answers possible.

5 Various answers possible.

6 1 The film might be a thriller
2 I might/might not go to the party
3 He might have got caught in traffic
4 I might go out on Saturday
5 They might not have time
6 She might have bought a new computer

7a dull – soundless – depressing – dreadful – dying

7b They are all negative.

Pages 114-115

1 Possible answers:
1 He receives a letter.
2 Very negative. That everything is decaying and dying.
3 His skin is pale. His eyes are large and watery. His hair is thin, long and fair.
4 That she has been very ill.
5 They are dark subjects but the light is strange in them.
6 He is obsessive, strange and appears mad.
7 Noises from the coffin and noises from the cellar.
8 It collapses into the lake.

2 1 nineteenth 2 romantic 3 originated 4 architecture 5 including 6 naturally

3 Across 1 terrifying 3 gloomy 6 sick 7 mystical 8 dull 9 ghostly
Down 2 enormous 4 decaying 5 wild 6 silent

Pages 116-117

Name: Edgar Poe
Date of Birth: January 19, 1809
Place of Birth: Boston, Massachusetts
Genres of Writing: poetry, gothic romantic fiction, detective stories, science fiction
Most Famous Poem: The Raven
Name of Wife: Virginia Clemm
Date of Death: 1849

Pages 118-119

1 Possible answers: Ligeia, The Tell-Tale Heart, The Fall of the House of Usher.

2-3 Various possible answers.

Pages 120-123

Various possible answers.

Page 124

1 Possible answers:

1 Yes. Because he thinks he is sane and he thinks his actions are rational.

2 Death and the end of time.

3 It is damp, dark, with a pit in the middle. The floor is slimy. It smells of fungus.

4 Being buried alive.

5 An enormous whirlpool.

6 They don't apply method.

7 To substitute the letter with a copy (on the pretext of collecting his pen).

8 He hates her.

9 She dies after being imprisoned in her coffin, alive.

2 **1** to groan **2** to dare **3** gloom **4** agile **5** to blackmail **6** to glow

Read for Pleasure: *Stories of Mystery and Suspense* 懸疑故事集

作　　者：	Edgar Allan Poe
改　　寫：	Janet Borsbey and Ruth Swan
繪　　畫：	Simone Rea
照　　片：	Shutterstock
責任編輯：	傅薇
封面設計：	涂慧
出　　版：	商務印書館（香港）有限公司
	香港筲箕灣耀興道 3 號東滙廣場 8 樓
	http://www.commercialpress.com.hk
發　　行：	香港聯合書刊物流有限公司
	香港新界大埔汀麗路 36 號中華商務印刷大廈 3 字樓
印　　刷：	中華商務彩色印刷有限公司
	香港新界大埔汀麗路 36 號中華商務印刷大廈 14 字樓
版　　次：	2016年9月第 1 版第 1 次印刷
	© 2016 商務印書館（香港）有限公司
	ISBN 978 962 07 0479 6
	Printed in Hong Kong
	版權所有　不得翻印